Dragon Reborn

Dragon Point #5

Eve Langlais

New York Times Bestseller

Copyright

Copyright © May 2017, Eve Langlais
Cover Art by Yocla Designs © June 2017
Edited by Devin Govaere, Literally Addicted to Detail, Amanda Pederick and Brieanna Robertson
Produced in Canada
Published by Eve Langlais
http://www.EveLanglais.com

E-ISBN: 978 1988 328 69 0
Print-ISBN: 978 1988 328 70 6

Prologue

The prisoner lay in a huddled heap, cowed in his cell. Oh, how the mighty had fallen.

It amused to watch the Golden pretender before his captivity, thinking he owned the throne. Ruling over his meager territory and the Septs as if he had the right.

None of them did.

The hatred burned brightly for those pompous dragons who thought they were so great. Not really in the grand scheme, more like silly little ants scurrying about not realizing what was coming.

He learned through the judicious use of pain just how insignificant he was. Now, the Golden heir, the one who thought he'd rule them all, would serve instead. He would help beget a new world order. *My order.*

But only once he took that final step.

He must give himself to me.

In the meantime, patience was required.

Soon. So soon, the world would burn. The day crept ever closer when humanity and dragons and all lesser creatures would bow or die.

The darkness of the cloak, a deep and lush fabric not found on Earth, flowed from the crown to past the toes, moving sinuously toward the door of the cell as if bound with smoke.

A wave of the hand and the locks disengaged. The barred entrance swung open, allowing access to the prison and its occupant.

The days where the Golden one would rise and attack were gone. Beaten into submission, and not all blows by the hand. The punishments that flailed the mind were so much better.

The body lay curled in the corner, head tucked, the tail wrapped around the body. Gold scales, dull and matted with filth and despair, rustled in agitation. Trembled in recognition.

Shivered in fear.

It had taken some time to break this one. Many pleasurable moments full of screams and pain.

But in the end, the man who'd once had it all, the dragon who thought he would inherit the throne, crumbled.

The first of many.

A hand reached out to touch the prize, the long, lithe fingers tipped in black nails. They brushed over the scales, vibrating at the power and magic contained within.

The captive dragon flinched, the head rearing back, causing the cloth collar around the neck to ripple the fine chain holding it down. Holding the beast prisoner.

From almost leader to pathetic ruin.

My secret weapon. But a weapon that couldn't be revealed too soon. Things still had to move into position, but when the time came, nothing would stop the coming war.

The world would suffer wrath and vengeance for what they'd done.

And burn.

Chapter One

Eschewing an appointment—those were for people with news of lesser importance—Deka sailed into her Aunt Zahra's office.

"Samael is missing," Deka announced to the Silvergrace matriarch before flopping into the club chair in front of the desk.

"Is that really the news you're using to justify barging in?" An arctic gaze pinned her.

"Well, yeah, it's important news. Samael is missing." The travesty. The horror. The where the hell is the future father of my babies? It was a big freaking chunk of news. "You're welcome." Now, Auntie could act to find him.

"I already knew he was gone. Remiel told me."

No surprise Zahra knew. As Sept matriarch, not much evaded her steely-eyed gaze.

"So when are we assembling the Sept to find him?" With Deka at the head of the posse, ready to save the day. Then he could thank her with a great big—

"We aren't assembling anything."

Say what? Hadn't she marshaled the Sept, mobilized their forces?

The reason why became clear. "I get it. You haven't launched a search party on account of Remiel wanting to find his brother himself." The love of a sibling, so cute—unless they tried to hone in on your dessert. Then you stabbed them with a fork.

"Actually, Remiel would prefer Samael never show his face again. He's still got some deep-seated issues."

Samael might have had a hand in keeping his brother locked in a pit with his memories wiped. But surely Remiel wouldn't hold a grudge forever?

Deka swung a leg over the arm of the chair and twirled a strand of hair. "Given the king is all happy now and ruling us all, surely he wouldn't mind Samael coming back. Maybe letting his little bro hook up with someone in the family." *Ahem. Me.*

"No," Auntie replied, not bothering to peek up from her stack of paperwork.

The abrupt reply didn't deter Deka. Auntie probably needed help in understanding the importance of finding Samael.

"Aren't you curious at all as to where he's gone?" Deka certainly couldn't handle not knowing. She'd been watching his house—the mansion vacant and up for sale since Remiel took over—and hadn't seen a single sign of Samael.

Rifling through his closet showed he hadn't packed a bag or taken his passport and that he didn't like to wear briefs. At least she didn't find any.

Just like me. Going commando meant less laundry, and Deka was all about keeping things simple for their staff.

With his house being a bust, she'd had to rely on electronic means to monitor him. As yet, she'd seen no activity on Samael's bank accounts, credit card, Netflix, or his favorite porn website. Nor had he placed any orders at his favorite restaurant for an extra large, double pepperoni, mushroom, olive, bacon, extra cheese with chipotle sauce smearing the base. Deka had left a few hundred in cash with the owner, along with orders to contact her if Samael called.

Extreme? Not really. Deka simply took her stalking seriously.

How else am I supposed to find my man?

"I really don't care if he's disappeared from public sight. More than likely, he's gone into hiding. Between his unholy union with that Crimson pretender and his treatment of our king, he's probably worried someone will assassinate him."

Over my dead body. I'll protect you, muffin.

"He's too valuable to kill." Even with his list of crimes, Golden blood coursed through Samael's veins—and he also had super sperm wearing glittery capes sleeping in his balls, waiting to shoot from his cannon dick. And, yes, she giggled each time she thought of the little bullet-headed fellows firing off into her vagina.

Genetics gave him, if not a free pass, at least a chance to live a long life—probably in captivity as a breeding bull.

Unless I save him. Once he became her mate, she'd keep him safe. Male dragons were rather rare and precious. Kind of like unicorns—which no one liked to admit had been eaten into extinction by dragons.

Shhh.

"Why this continued interest in him?" Zahra lifted her head and stared at Deka, the directness of her gaze unnerving. However, Deka had been the object of many stern gazes in her life and simply shrugged.

"It just seems like we should be paying more

attention. What if the wrong sorts got their hands on him?"

In other words, what if some hussy with designs on his body dug in her claws. Then Deka would have to murder her, and that might start a war, which would be fun but messy, especially since the humans now knew that dragons existed. She'd heard there'd been a rise in demand for giant crossbows that fired harpoon-sized arrows.

It meant the training all dragons went through had been amped up a notch. They weren't being complacent about their safety and survival. Ever since they'd been almost wiped out, they'd learned how to survive.

And fight.

"I really don't care if another Sept snatches him." The matriarch arched a brow. "Don't tell me you haven't gotten over your obsession with that man."

"He's mine." Of that, Deka had no doubt. From the moment she'd first seen the guy, his golden hair perfectly combed—in need of a ruffle—and the smirk—that totally said, "take off your clothes"— she'd wanted him.

But someone was telling Deka she couldn't have him.

It's not up to her to decide.

Zahra still blathered. "You do realize with the return of the Golden king we no longer need to enforce breeding protocols. You're free to mate, or not, as you choose."

"Then I choose him."

A heavy sigh. "I would prefer, and I know your mother agrees with me, that you select someone else. He's got bad blood."

"Golden blood."

"He's tainted. You've read the reports we filched from Parker's labs."

Ah, yes, good old Parker, the wolf shifter who'd outed cryptozoids to the humans. Now, everyone suspected his or her neighbor of being some kind of enhanced being. The sale on silver and shotguns had shot through the roof. The zappers in the yard got bigger as folks tried to prevent any fairies from taking over their green space. And swords, along with armor, were making a comeback as wannabe heroes thought to go on quests to find dragon treasure.

As a side note, armor was the number one reason most quests ended abruptly. The most common of that being drowning.

Deka realized her aunt was staring and shrugged. "I know what the reports say." She'd read every single medical one. Her mother surely meant for her to check them out, given she'd put them in her special safe. "Samael D'Ore is definitely the brother of one very majestic Remiel D'Ore. But he's not a full-breed like the king. The maternal half he inherited makes him part of the Gold Sept."

"It's the other half that worries me," admitted Zahra. "There is something about that boy…" She pursed her lips and pointed a manicured finger at Deka. "Forget Samael. Find yourself another man. You can even consort with a *human*"—no mistaking the sneer— "if you'd like. Your mother has been working with the other Septs' scientists to figure out the serum to help transition the wyverns. A few have ascended into their true shape."

"Which is awesome."

It truly was. For centuries, the dragons had

enforced brutal breeding programs to ensure their continuity. It led to a few cross-eyed cousins and blathering idiots. Male dragons were few and far between, and while humans tasted delicious—and not just in a basted-over-the-fire-with-rosemary-and-garlic kind of way as endorsed by Aunt Claudia—they couldn't make real dragon babies. Progeny between a dragon and a human were known as wyverns, sterile hybrids that did nothing to continue the family bloodlines. Unless they got injected with a special dragon cocktail to force them to ascend.

Blah, blah, all kinds of science. The details didn't apply to her because she planned to make babies with a dragon. A Golden dragon...

"Forget that tainted misfit." Zahra still shook that finger. Deka's tummy rumbled for French fries. "Or face the consequences. You know the king has said we are to leave his brother alone."

Forbidden. Was there any tastier treasure?

"But—"

"Oh no, you don't." Zahra narrowed her gaze at Deka. "I know that look. You will stop that train of thought this instant. And I will ease one fear. Samael will not be touched. The Septs have been warned of what will happen should they capture Samael and try to use him to steal the throne. And that includes us."

A ruthless king. And a handsome Gold one at that. It was enough to make a girl swoon, especially after Remiel's first throne speech, broadcasted via Skype, to the Septs around the world. It was a great speech, short, to the point, and ended with, "Betray me and die."

It got resounding applause. Who didn't want a tough ruler who declared that any who disobeyed would find themselves crushed to a pulp? Remiel was arrogantly powerful like that, and Brand's sister was super lucky to have him as her mate.

Deka was also green with envy. She wanted a man who could pulverize his enemies like a bug, too. Not that she wasn't capable of smooshing them herself, but think of how much fun couples night would be. Smiting some foes, maybe getting some treasures for the hoard—you could never have too many Pokémon collectibles—grabbing a hoagie, and then sex.

Good sex. The kind that didn't have a gal worrying she'd accidentally put her lover in traction.

Again.

Stupid Silvergrace family lawyer now had her make potential partners sign a waiver before she got wild with them. It tended to kill the mood.

"Why does this say I promise not to sue if, during the course of sexual intercourse, you break my bones or rupture my organs?"

"Just a precaution."

"Is it a precaution to list side effects such as blood in my urine, paralysis, and death?"

Many walked at that point; some even ran. It meant her poor vibrator was going through a lot of batteries lately and would soon join her collection of plastic penises that couldn't keep up with her appetite.

But I bet a big, strong Golden dragon could.

Now if only her matriarch would agree.

Deka amped up her argument. "What if it's not one of the Septs who takes him but that freak-ass bitch who pretended to be Anastasia for a while?"

Some mysterious figure with glowing red eyes had messed with dragon politics. They should be hunting her ass down. Instead, the Septs had retreated and closed ranks, fearful of getting into a fight. No one wanted to join the fate of the Crimson Sept, decimated in number and dropping from second most powerful to last.

Zahra slid a sheaf of papers aside in order to begin signing the next set. "We've no reason to believe that entity has any interest in us any longer."

"No interest? She gave us a head." Literally. They'd yet to come across the body.

"The head of our enemy. A fitting gift, if you ask me."

Deka kind of agreed, still, all this no-you-can't-go-find-the-hottest-thing-since-spicy-margarita-night-at-the-pub shit was ruining her fun.

A heavy sigh left Deka. "I don't understand why you're not more worried."

Zahra braced her hands on her desk and leaned forward. "Dragons don't worry. Especially not about other beings. Everyone knows there is none greater or more powerful than our kind. We are the top of the food chain, the true leaders of this world, and now that our king has returned, we shall take our rightful place."

"Our rightful place better not mean wearing skirts and shit," Deka mumbled.

"If you ask me, the day women shortened their skirts and started wearing pants was when things got messed up. Back in my day—"

"When they'd just learned to make fire."

"—a lady did not chase after a man."

"That's not what I heard. I heard you tackled Uncle and told him you'd tell everyone he got beaten by a girl unless he took you to the debutante ball."

Aunt Zahra glared. "I see your mother has been yapping again. She obviously remembers things differently. And it has no bearing on the here and now. When our king truly rules the world, you will curtsy and wear a dress."

"I guess if it's ankle-length, no one can bitch about my hairy legs."

"There will be no hairy legs. You will shave."

"You don't have to shave in Europe," Deka muttered. "Wish I lived there."

"If you think it's so wonderful, then perhaps you should plan a trip abroad."

"I don't want to go. I've got stuff to do here." Deka crossed her arms and sulked.

"Things like hunting down a man who doesn't want to be found and vexing me?" Auntie arched a perfectly manicured brow. "I say enough of that. You are going to Europe. It will do you some good to immerse yourself in a new culture and visit some of the other Silver Sept branches. The Belleargents in Paris come to mind."

"Do I have to go to Paris?" Deka wrinkled her nose.

"Yes. That is an order."

"If you say so, boss." Deka bounced up from her chair and headed for the door.

"That's it? You aren't going to argue a little longer?" Auntie sounded puzzled.

"First, you're giving me heck for not listening to you, and now that I am obeying promptly, you're still getting annoyed." Deka rolled her eyes. "I can't ever do anything right. Maybe I should stay home."

"Pack your bags! I am booking you on the first flight to France. Don't you dare miss it."

"Yes, ma'am," said quite somberly, at odds with the smile on her lips. Good thing she had her back to Aunt Zahra. She'd wonder why Deka was so excited about going to Europe, which coincidentally was where a certain crate, with a manifest bearing Anastasia's name—dated after her death—had been shipped.

A box that she was pretty certain had a man inside.

My man.

And she was going to find him. Even better, she had permission. Of a sort.

Auntie says I have to go to Europe. Wouldn't hurt to look up an old friend while visiting.

Bouncing out of the office and heading to her room to pack—more like zip up her duffel bag since she'd prepared it ahead of time; Auntie was so predictable—she ran into her cousin Babette.

"Why do you have the grin that says you ate Farmer Brown's prized cow again?"

"Ew, what do you mean *again*?" Deka's nose wrinkled. "I digested and pooped that thing out ages ago. Nothing left to eat." And dragons were much too refined to eat rotting corpses, and that included zombies.

"Something's got you excited. Spill."

"Auntie is sending me to Europe."

"Europe?" Babette's voice rose. "Lucky heifer. How come I never get sent to cool places? Instead, it's 'Babette, ask Cameron to pick up my prescription.' 'Babette, make sure the staff detail my Bentley.'"

"Babette, stop talking about yourself in the third person."

Her cousin and best friend wrinkled her nose. "Nope, because I am so great," she sang.

"What'd you do?"

"I made Mother guzzle a bottle of wine last night." Babette grinned with pride.

"That's not a great accomplishment."

"It was a two-liter bottle, and she wouldn't share. She did, however, agree to let me dye her hair. I might have miscalculated the colors."

"So you're the reason she looks like a rainbow barfed on her head."

"Just helping her change up her style, but did I get any thanks?"

"No!" they shouted in unison then giggled.

"So why is Auntie sending you to Europe?" Babette asked as she followed Deka through the vast mansion they called home.

White and gray marble, painted walls, and gilded molding gave the halls they passed through a rich elegance.

The red crayon on a lower panel with the scribbled words, "Polly is a poopy head," reminded Deka of when she and Babette had been young and raising hell.

Not that they weren't still raising hell. They just did it more maturely now by writing messages in the sky or having it plastered on the Jumbotron at ball games.

"Aunt Zahra thinks I should immerse myself in the culture that is France since I'm already half-French, what with my unshaven pits and legs."

"Did you explain it's because you ran out of razors and keep forgetting to ask Cameron to put them on the list?"

"Details," Deka replied with a lofty wave of her hand.

"I'm surprised you agreed to go. What happened to finding your mate? You know, the one who doesn't even realize you're alive?"

A scowl pulled Deka's expression. "He was kind of busy at the time. I'm sure, had we enjoyed

some proper time together"—naked and in her bed—
"he'd have realized we were meant to be."

"More like realized you needed to be committed. The man is bad news."

"I know." It was one of his more appealing qualities.

"So does this trip mean you've given up."

"Of course, not."

"So you're going to try and get out of it." Babette nodded her head.

"Nope. I am going to be on that plane for Paris."

"Hold on a second." Babette's brow creased. "You shouldn't be agreeable about this. Why aren't you fighting?" A light bulb went off. "Holy shit, you're still looking for him. In Europe!"

"Shush!" Deka hissed, her finger over her lips. "Don't let Auntie hear you. She'll forbid me from going."

"And? Since when does that stop you?"

"It doesn't." Deka shrugged. Forbidding a dragoness was like putting a pie out to cool and telling hungry faces and grabby hands not to touch it. It was gone in under five minutes. "Going with permission, though, means all expenses paid."

Babette's gaze narrowed. "Take me with you."

"Sorry, cuz. You know what they say. Two's a couple. Three's—"

"A ménage."

A snicker escaped Deka. And this was why she loved Babette. Like a sister, not a sister wife. "Sorry, but I am not sharing this dick."

"Ugh." Babette gagged. "You know how I feel about sausage. It's only good for breakfast and if served with bacon. But pie on the other hand…"

Babette's lips rounded in pleasure. "I love me some fresh pie."

"Lots of flavors where I'm going," Deka mused aloud. Having an extra set of eyes along might not hurt. After all, anything badass enough to kidnap a Golden dragon might be a *soupçon* difficult to deal with. *Look at me, using French words already.*

"How do we convince Auntie to send me with you? You know she says we're troublemakers when we work together."

"Because we are." Way to state the obvious.

"I know. I don't know why they think that's a bad thing." Babette smirked. "Remember the last time we went away together?"

"Don't even think of it," Deka hastened to say. "She'll ban us both from going if you remind her of that incident." The one that left her unable to enter Canada.

And, Deka might add, it took a lot to get banned by Canada. The terms of her banishment precluded her from speaking about it. Needless to say, she couldn't look at poutine without giggling.

"Good times," Babette said with a sigh.

"Yes, they were." Deka turned thoughtful for a moment—it almost hurt. "Why not tell her you're thinking of taking French as a second language."

"Yeah, that won't fly. I used that excuse when I told her to stock the pond with frogs."

"I remember that. They were delicious." Especially when battered and deep-fried.

"Maybe I should pretend to be a caring cousin and tell Auntie you shouldn't be sent alone."

At that, they both giggled.

In the end, Babette simply told Aunt Zahra that she thought the local police chief was in love with her, and as soon as she got rid of the husband, they planned to run away together and start a hippy commune in the desert dedicated to the spiritual pursuit of peyote smoking.

In short order, Babette was commanded to join Deka on a European vacation, first class—which meant they got to drive the suits sitting with them nuts—and were assigned a luxurious suite at the Four Seasons Hotel George V.

Only the best for Silvergrace daughters.

But Deka didn't plan to use the hotel room for long because, if her plan worked, she'd soon be with Samael.

"Don't worry, stud muffin. I'm coming for you." And it was Babette who added the ominous laugh to her statement.

Chapter Two

Arriving in a strange city where it seemed everyone spoke another language might have daunted anyone else.

Not Deka. Whatever the doorman yelled at her was probably something like, *Hey, sexy, let me get your ride.*

No need. She found one. The cab pulled up in front of the portico. How fortuitous she made it into the car first.

The lady wearing too much makeup—to the point it caked in her wrinkles— shook her fist. As if it were Deka's fault the human was too slow with her walker to jump in.

The driver, a beefy fellow in a turban and a luxurious beard, turned to look at her. He jabbered something. She assumed it was along the lines, of, *Hey, pretty lady, where might I take you on this lovely day?*

Who needed to learn a second language when she could just decipher expressions and intent?

"Take me to a museum. The big one with lots of old stuff." Because, according to the manifest she'd borrowed—without permission because a Silvergrace shouldn't have to ask—a museum was the final destination of the crate she tracked.

The man yelled and gestured some more while the doorman ensured her door was firmly shut and locked by tugging on it. Their combined niceness made her dig into her purse and toss some money over the seat.

"Museum. Pronto." Which was French for fast. Or was that Italian?

Her driver obviously thought highly of her tip because he threw the car into gear and sped off like a bat out of hell. He didn't believe in speed limits, gestured at drivers who dared get in the way, and sometimes had to brake on a dime, causing some whiplash. Her kind of driver.

At the speed he was going, she'd make it to her destination in record time because for once, Deka was being responsible and following a clue. As for Babette, Deka had left her snoring in bed, the mimosa she'd fed her cousin knocking her out. Her cousin never could handle champagne and roofies together.

But Deka didn't mind going off on her own. She preferred it, as a matter of fact, because she didn't want anyone else homing in on her man when she found him.

The cab whipped to a stop, and the man pointed to the meter. She showered him with more bills and was rewarded with a beaming smile.

Exiting the cab, even her spoiled ass was impressed by the size of the buildings she faced. Bigger than Auntie Zahra's mansion—which she ensured she noted in her Snapchat story as Deka posed with it in the background—it sported statues of people instead of gargoyles on the roof.

She wondered what the gargoyle guild had to say about that.

The giant glass pyramid in front of the museum proved interesting from an architectural point of view. It also would have looked better with a gargoyle perched at the very top.

Perhaps she'd leave that suggestion in their box.

The ticket to get inside—the nerve charging her an admission—took some more of her cash.

The vastness of the place impressed, although the number of old things on display did make her wrinkle her nose. Would it kill them to modernize some of the older stuff?

Ugly paintings abounded, as did statues missing body parts. The male statues, for the most part, could have used a hand job to make them a little more presentable. Who thought it was a good idea to carve them after having obviously taken a cold shower?

Deka wandered through room after room, posing with the *Mona Lisa*—ass in the air, twerking to a live Facebook post—cupping a statue with sizeable balls, and even did cartwheels through one long hall.

But she didn't find a dragon.

Not a single one. Not even a smell hinting at one.

Which was why she finally let the guards catch up to her.

They grabbed her by the arms, but when a dragoness didn't want to move, nobody, especially not two puny humans, could budge her. Which was why, a moment later, a slender man in a suit sporting a porn-stache appeared, looking most anxious to speak with her.

"Mizz, you haz to go," he said with an adorable lisp.

"Not until you take me to my dragon."

The man blinked at her, obviously in awe of her perfect pronunciation.

"Zer iz no dragonz here," he said, again doing strange things to the English language.

"Zou lie!" she declared, getting into the game.

"Leave, or I will call ze police."

"Will they use handcuffs?" she asked. "I love a little bondage. But my future mate might not appreciate me dallying before our wedding. So, instead of trying to tempt me, why not tell me where he is?"

"Where who iz?" asked the short man.

"Samael. My future husband. About yay big." She extended her arms. "Kind of scaly. Looks like a dragon on account he *is* a dragon."

Again, he blinked at her. She wondered if perhaps his hearing aid needed new batteries.

She spoke more slowly and made sure he could see her lips. "I know you know about him. Everyone in the world knows about Samael and his brother Remiel. They were on television."

"Zer iz no dragonz here."

The rebuttal brought a sigh. "Now listen, I know that a crate containing my fiancé was delivered to your museum. Just tell me where it went, and I'll leave. Don't tell me and…" She leaned forward and drew forth enough of her inner beast to make her eyes glow green. "And you will get to meet your first dragon. Did I mention I have a really long tail?" She glanced around the gallery full of fragile vases and glass cases.

His eyes widened, showing proper appreciation. "I know not of zis package, but if madame will come wiz me, we shall check. And zen you will leave, *oui?*"

"I only want my stud muffin. So, lead the way, little man." She wrenched her arms free and followed

The Suit as he practically jogged in his haste to please her.

Such nice people these French.

Alas, he couldn't do much to help her. He did locate the shipping receipt for the crate; however, a search for the box proved futile.

"It zeemz to be mizzing." Frenchie appeared quite perturbed.

She patted his arm. "Don't take it too hard. I'm sure you'll find a nice job after they fire you." Just not with any Silvergrace companies. Really, how hard was it to track a mysterious box—which wasn't supposed to exist—that had disappeared?

With the museum leading to a dead end, Deka had to reevaluate. Thinking was hard work that required a box full of croissants, a baguette, and a bottle of red wine. She dumped them on Babette, who woke with a snort and a line of drool hanging from the corner of her mouth.

"Whazzup?" she asked blearily.

"Holy shit, Babette. One night here and you're speaking like a native."

A shove propelled Babette to a sitting position, and the bottle of wine rolled precariously close to the edge of the bed. Good thing it was empty. Deka had found herself thirsty after those two hours of hard searching.

Scrubbing her face, Babette managed to focus her gaze. "Where have you been?"

"Chasing down my fiancé."

"You're engaged? I take it you found him, then?"

"Not exactly. But it's only a matter of time, and when I do, I'm sure he won't want a long engagement."

Babette blinked, much like Louis—the little man in the suit—had, and Deka had to wonder if there was something in the air that made people incapable of comprehending simple logic.

"Did you find any clues as to his whereabouts?" Babette asked finally.

"Nope. But I did bring you breakfast."

Babette leaned over and opened the box of croissants. Six flavors inside. "Why is there a bite gone from each one?"

"I was testing them, of course." Deka rolled her eyes. "You'll be glad to know they're delicious."

"So, what's next?" Babette asked, stuffing her face with flaky goodness.

"I don't know. Louie said he'd call me if he got any news on the box."

"Louie being?"

"My new friend at the museum. You should hear his nickname for me. Ze crazy bitch. The accent is adorable. I might get him to record it for me as the ringtone for the family."

"Where are we searching next?"

"Next, we are going to pay a visit to our long-lost family."

"They aren't exactly lost, given we have an address."

"Whatever. Dress to impress as Auntie would say, because I hear the French side of the Silver Sept is snooty."

The French cousins were also less than impressed with the American cousins who showed up on their doorstep wearing designer jeans, ripped up both legs to the crotch; corsets that displayed their natural bosoms; and high-top sneakers.

Utterly jealous of our style. Deka held her head

high. Aunt J held hers higher.

Aunt Josephine also looked down her aquiline nose at Deka when she said, "Have you seen a box with my fiancé inside?"

That got her a sniff, which translated to a snooty no.

"What about some psycho being with glowing red eyes from another dimension—"

"We don't know if it's from another dimension," Babette interrupted in a whisper.

"It body-snatched Anastasia. Of course, it came from elsewhere," Deka said with a roll of her eyes.

"Aunt Zahra said we shouldn't talk about it."

"Holy shit, you're right. For all we know, Aunt J here is a body snatcher, too." A razor-sharp stare failed to crack her stoic demeanor. "I'm gonna have to check you over."

Aunt J didn't appreciate Deka's determination to discover whether she was real or not—good news, the face didn't peel off like a mask. Bad news? Much like other Sept parties, Deka and Babette were tossed on the street, whereupon, Deka shouted, "If you see a box with a dragon inside, or see my fiancé period, give me a ring. I'm at the hotel." And then, just in case Aunt J didn't know the address, she recited it loudly. Twice.

Slam. The door held up splendidly.

"And that's that," Deka said with a satisfied grin. "We have now done our familial duty. Not our fault we didn't get along."

"Leaving us free to do whatever we like." Babette giggled. "You are devious, heifer. So devious."

"I know." It was a gift.

No one accosted them on the way back to the hotel, even though they went through some pretty dark alleys.

Paris wasn't as fun as expected and not for lack of trying.

Deka spent the next few days visiting more museums, popping by to see Louis, who aimed a crossbow at her—the man did love to play, although if he were going to shoot arrows, he really should learn to catch them when she tossed them back.

Everywhere Deka went, she asked loudly about her missing dragon and ensured she gave everyone she met her contact info.

If it weren't for the fact that Deka couldn't find Samael, she would have called her vacation in Paris a success. She got banned from the Eiffel Tower for taking a selfie on it—topless. Kicked out of all kinds of restaurants because, apparently, patrons did not want to share their meal with her so she could make up her mind. Even the hotel sent her an ultimatum to stop calling the kitchen to ask if they had King Albert in the can.

With every lead and corner she peeked in coming up empty, she almost began to wonder if she'd fail. A first, and not an achievement she wanted to start a collection of.

Given her shenanigans weren't exactly discreet, Auntie Zahra heard of her exploits and, jealous because she couldn't join Deka on her vacation, ordered her home.

I can't go home. Not until I find him.

Time was running out, and there were still so many bars she'd yet to get thrown out of.

But, finally, all her work bore fruit.

As she staggered out of a tavern, which served

the most delicious sidecars, into the alley where someone had smashed all the lights, she noticed a distinct lack of smell.

Which usually would be a good thing in a garbage-stinking alley, except she was looking right at a rabble of men and women. Tough-looking wyverns wearing leather and chains.

"You the woman looking for Samael?" asked the big bald dude at the head of them.

Excitement bubbled inside. "Indeed, I am."

"You need to come with us."

"I'd be delighted," she exclaimed, her smile wide and welcoming. "I was wondering what a gal had to do to get abducted around here." She held out her hands. "Take me to your leader."

Hold on, stuff muffin. I'm on my way.

Chapter Three

A chattering feminine voice woke him.

"Mind hurrying it up there, minion of darkness. I'm excited to see my dungeonesque quarters. Although, I really wish you'd let me keep my phone. How am I supposed to Snapchat about my incarceration? Do you have any idea the number of views I'd get? Not to mention the jealousy factor because I went on a European vacation and was abducted by someone with a castle."

The bright sound in this place of pain and darkness had him lifting his head. A chain rattled with the movement, a discordant chime reminding him of his status.

Just a prisoner. A broken shell of the man he used to be.

How long since he'd lived on top of the world? His every whim catered to. His every vice fulfilled. Women, booze, riches, and more…he had it all.

But that was before.

How long now? The days of torture and vile potions melded together, making it seem as if an eternity had passed. Now, he only remembered the good times in his dreams because, when he woke, he lived a nightmare.

How dramatic.

Shut up.

He'd earned the right to his melancholy.

Then do something about it.

The inner voice didn't seem to recognize the futility in trying.

Just like the woman skipping down the hall still harbored a joyful outlook. That would soon change.

He roused himself enough to venture a peek through the bars at the far end of his cavernous prison and thus saw the bare legs of a woman in a short dress as she skipped by.

"Is it this one?" She pointed to his cell. "Or that one?" She gestured to the one across from it. Onwards she went, still talking. "Oooh, that one has rats. Can I have that one?"

"Halt," gargled the jailor, a vile creature he'd come to know during his incarceration. Half slug, half more revolting slug, the jailor was the one who'd dragged him to his punishment.

"But I haven't seen the ones on the end," the woman said in a pouty voice much too cute for this place. "Mother always advises to ask for a corner room. Less noise that way. Do any of the cells come with windows?"

Did the foolish female not grasp the severity of her situation? How dare she sound so cheerful?

How dare the brightness of the sound warm something cold and dormant inside him!

"Come back here. Those cells aren't for the likes of you." The jailor jangled keys in front of his cell.

No, not a roommate. He wanted to wallow alone in his misery.

But she sounds so tasty, the beast inside

whispered. *And we are so hungry for meat.* The rats she so admired no longer strayed anywhere near him.

"That one?" The woman reappeared, back turned to him, her platinum hair touching the tops of her shoulders, the skirt of her dress hugging a pert ass. "It's hu-u—u-ge." Followed by a snicker.

The silly woman joked. Did she not notice the prison cell? Then again, perhaps she was fooled by the bars with their misleading dull appearance that should have been easy to bend, except they burned when he touched the metal alloy.

What is it? Whatever the bars were made of, it acted like kryptonite. He'd learned the painful, blistering way.

The cell across from him had the same kind of bars, and now it would have a new occupant. Someone like him. Someone with a voice he dimly recognized.

She cornered me after the rooftop encounter with the wyverns and said, "Hey, good-looking, wanna get wild?"

He'd not taken her up on her offer at the time, too preoccupied with his brother stealing the limelight.

But now she was here, a part of his nightmare.

There's nothing I can do.

Aren't you even going to try?

What's the point?

While he argued with himself, she whirled to face his cell, and he noted her slim ankles leading up to toned calves.

Calves made for wrapping around my waist.

She couldn't stay still, bouncing on the balls of her feet as she stared right at him. His imagination, surely. No one could see into the darkest pocket he'd found to hide in.

His gaze strayed upward to see the pink fabric of her dress smudged with grime, the front low-cut and hugging her breasts.

The cleavage almost managed to rouse a hunger he'd not felt in a while.

He couldn't see hands, as her wrists were tethered behind her back, and having been in the same position once before, he knew those shackles were made of the same material as the bars but lined with fabric. It prevented the skin from burning on contact, yet proved impossible to wrench apart.

The woman wearing them didn't seem to mind. She rocked on her heels as the jailor shoved the first of three keys into the locks of the cell across from his. It had to be done quickly, one after another, in order for the door to spring open. It meant that picking one did shit because he couldn't pick the other two quickly enough. Usually, as he worked on the third, the spring connecting them together would snap, and the locks would slam back with a frustrating click.

Also known as the sound of failure. He had quite a collection of those now.

She peeked closer, her nose almost touching the bars. "Who's in the other cell?"

Despite him remaining still in the shadows cloaking the far end of his prison, she'd noted his presence. More like smelled it. He'd not bathed in a while. A good thing because cleanliness usually meant a visit from *her*.

"Don't you worry about him. He don't say much since the suzerain broke him."

"Broke him how?" she asked, turning away.

"You'll soon see." The ominous chuckle sent a shiver down his spine because he knew. Knew the pain awaiting her.

Save her.

Not my problem. He wasn't a hero before this all happened, and he wasn't about to become one now.

"In you go." The jailor went to shove her, only she moved more quickly, skipping into her new home and twirling to exclaim, "This is just dreadful." She grinned. "I love it. Babette is going to be so mad she didn't go out drinking with me. She won't be able to say she was caught by some evil Suzie—"

"Suzerain." The title his captor insisted on. It proved easier to give in after repeated uses of the word bitch left him a bruised mess.

"Whatever. This is epic. Although it would be more epic with a camera, hint, hint."

The jailor didn't reply, instead choosing to slam the door of the cell shut. It didn't need the keys to automatically lock with a loud click.

"Turn around. Give me your hands. I'll remove the cuffs," the jailor ordered.

The manacles only came off after they were safely stored in the cell.

"What if I want to keep them?"

The jailor growled. "Don't be difficult."

"Or what? You'll spank me. My fiancé probably wouldn't appreciate that. So, since you insist." She whirled and presented her hands through the bars then hissed as the jailor yanked on them, forcing them against the metal, burning her skin as he removed the cuffs.

"Damn, Jabba. Those bars are made of some legit dracinore. I thought that stuff was extinct."

"You thought wrong," was the reply. "You should probably rest. The suzerain will come for you later."

Was it only him, or did those words deserve a dun-dun-dun musical score?

The plodding steps of the jailor receded, followed by a distant thud as the door to the dungeon slammed shut. Alone again in almost perfect darkness but for the one flickering torch in the hall.

But you're not alone anymore.

"Yoo hoo. You can come out now," she sang.

Answer her.

Why? What can I say? Oh, hey, welcome to my nightmare. Hope you have a high threshold for pain, not that it matters. The suzerain will have you sobbing in no time flat.

Whiner.

Fuck off.

"Would it kill you to say hello?"

Wait, that wasn't his mind speaking but her.

She approached the bars. "There's no point in hiding. I know you're there."

He held still.

"Listen, I understand you're overwhelmed. I mean, it's not every day your future intended, who is drop-dead gorgeous, comes to your rescue. Some men might find that emasculating, but I'm sure you're evolved enough to not care."

Rescue me? A dragon did not need a female to come to his aid.

Have you not noticed your current dilemma?

What part of fuck off do you not understand?

"Just in case you suffered some kind of amnesia, it's me, Deka Silvergrace. We met a while back when you were in your evil overlord phase."

Ever get the distinct impression someone wouldn't shut up unless you answered?

With a mental sigh, he shrank on himself, compacting all his lovely body into the confined form of a human male. A dirty, stinking one, sporting a ragged growth of beard and no clothes. He kept to the shadows and not just because the collar around his neck tethered him. He wasn't about to let the woman who practically shone with a silvery inner light see how far he'd fallen.

"What is that smell?" she exclaimed.

"Shut up."

Now there's a way to say hello to a beautiful woman.

You can shut up, too.

These conversations with himself were driving him a little crazy.

"It speaks!" she crowed. "All hail, Samael. The smelly, evil overlord."

"I said shut up!" He lunged to his feet and approached the bars, body bristling, the chain rattling along with him. He made sure to keep clear of it lest it burn. He had enough scars.

His lunge brought him out of the shadows, and her eyes widened.

"Holy Captain Caveman. You know, stud muffin, I thought you were hot before, but this whole untamed thing you've got going is pretty sexy, too."

"Why do you persist in blathering? Do you have any idea of the gravity of the situation?"

"I thought gravity was constant all over the Earth. That's what my science teacher told me. Or was that false? Is there a conspiracy afoot to keep us from really knowing the true gravity that exerts a force on a body? Is that why my scale at home always has me ten pounds lighter than at the doctor's?"

The direction her mind took was so drastic, he didn't dignify it with a reply. "How did you get here? How did they capture you?"

"In an alley outside a club. I thought for sure

they'd come after me at the hotel, though. I even made sure to leave the balcony doors open every night. But no, they were so cliché about their abduction."

"You sound as if you expected it."

"Well, duh. I didn't go around Paris leaving clues everywhere for nothing, you know."

"We're in Paris?" He'd wondered at his location, given the last thing he recalled was a warehouse, then the inside of a box, then this cell.

"Yes, Paris, the city of love. It will add a romantic element to our story when we tell our children."

That rendered him speechless. "What the fuck did you say?"

"Oooh, listen to you using bad words. Good thing Aunt Yolanda isn't here. She won't care if you're the Golden king's brother. She'd make you swallow some of that nasty oil. Which, I will add, is kind of dumb because I usually spit it out and say something worse."

He couldn't follow her, so he didn't bother trying. "Why did you want to get captured?"

"To find you, of course. I told my family you were mine, but they wouldn't help. Which is cool. I mean, I can totally rescue you myself. So cheer up, my sexy stud muffin. I'm here to take you home."

Chapter Four

Poor guy. He was overwhelmed with emotion. Gasping and choking in his cell.

She grabbed the bars, determined to be with him, only to suck in a breath as the metal singed the skin on her hands. She snatched her poor abused appendages back and glared at the offending bars.

Stupid dracinore. She'd learned about the metal at her mother's knee. Xylia, the Silver Sept's resident alchemist, possessed a tiny sample. Deka still remembered the burning lesson when she'd grabbed it from her mother's worktable with her chubby fist and popped it into her mouth—she'd gone through a stage of swallowing anything that her mother told her not to touch. It led to a few visits to the ER and some X-rays that she'd framed on the walls of her hoard.

Mother had made her spit it out then gargle a saline solution to neutralize the effects. Deka remembered trying not to cry—because, according to cousin Gilly, only sissy babies cried.

Holding Deka on her lap and rocking her, Mother had proceeded to explain why it hurt so badly—worse even than the bleach she'd swallowed in an attempt to make her blood the same color as her hair.

"That chunk of metal is dracinore, baby girl. The most dangerous metal known to our kind."

"It burns," she lisped.

"It does. And it's harder to recover from because it affects us on a cellular level, impeding our rapid healing ability. You can blame this metal for our downfall. Someone gave large amounts of dracinore to our enemies, and they made swords and arrows out of it. Not expecting it, we fell by the hundreds to their weapons."

"Why do that?" she asked. Why' being her favorite word ever, along with, 'Hey, Babette, wanna jump off this?'

"Why else but to kill the greatest species ever. The other races have always envied our kind. Humans, especially, feared us. Rather than serve us as the superior species, they chose to murder us into extinction. They almost succeeded. But despite our grievous losses, we rallied. We became wilier than the hunters. For decades we hid from the deadly weapons, made the humans think we were extinct. But meanwhile, we plotted. Our ancestors infiltrated the castles of those who attacked us. They collected all the dracinore weapons. Every last one of them."

"Where are the swords now?" little Deka asked— because a mighty blade to smite anyone, especially that hateful cousin Peter with his braying laugh, sounded like just the thing.

"Gone. A person with magic opened a rift and tossed that nasty metal back into the dimension from whence it came. Except for this one piece." Mother held it up with tongs.

Then slapped Deka's hand when she grabbed for it.

The lesson from it all? Don't eat rocks, and supposedly only teeny-tiny pieces of dracinore remained.

Until now. Cue the ominous music.

Apparently, someone had access to the dimension where it came from and had brought some back because the bars of her cell were covered in it.

The worst part? The stuff didn't just burn. It had some strange magical attribute that made shifting into her dragon almost impossible and nullified a dragon's strength. Even if she'd been able to bear the painful touch, she wouldn't be able to bend the bars.

It meant that, for the moment, she was— gasp—no better than a human.

The shame. Speaking of shame…someone in the cell across from her didn't have any.

"What happened to your clothes?" Not that she minded his nakedness. Despite his Grizzly Adams appearance, Samael had nothing to hide. His lean body—leaner than she liked to see—boasted nicely toned muscles, and he was rather… "Mind moving your hands? I'm trying to check you out."

He cupped his groin and glared. "I didn't give you permission to ogle."

"Are you going to try and give me orders?" She clapped her hands and bounced. "How exciting. Mother and the aunties do that all the time, which means I'm predisposed to disobey. But with you, I don't know if I should listen and please you." Wink. "Or disobey and have you punish me." Wink. Wink. The possibilities almost melted her girly bits.

"Do you ever shut up?"

"When my mouth is full. Why not move that hand so we can see if you have enough to accomplish that."

The black look didn't seem keen on cooperating.

How adorable. Much better than the woebegone heap she'd noted upon first entering the dungeon. A prison that came straight out of a B-movie, and her without the ability to take a picture for her memory album.

"So when do we get fed around here? I am starving. The bar I got drunk at didn't even have peanuts. Talk about cheap."

"We get one bowl of gruel a day."

"Gruel, as in soupy kind of oatmeal stuff with chunks." She shook her head. "That won't do. I didn't build this body on diet crap." She gestured to her frame, pleased to note he admired her properly. "We'll have to order in. Are you in the mood for pizza or Chinese?"

"You do realize this is a prison. We can't call out for food. Nor make demands. This isn't fucking Club Med."

"As if Mother would let me stay there. Club Med is for humans." Dragons stayed at special resorts, the kind that offered scale scrubbing and fang sharpening.

"I'm done dealing with you." He turned to walk away, showing off those superb glutes of his. He acknowledged her admiring whistle with a finger. Probably the one he planned to pleasure her with when they escaped their dastardly cells.

How sweet of him to tease her.

Now as to their escape…

I might have bitten off more than I can chew.

Nothing wrong with a big mouthful, and the joke was on him. She'd already seen his equipment when he wasn't paying attention. At repose, his dick was a thick slumbering beast. She wondered what it would take to get it to rouse and ravish.

Despite his dismissal—which, hello, she'd not condoned, so it didn't count—she continued to speak.

"What do they offer for entertainment around here?"

Dead silence.

"Are there any other prisoners, or is it just you

and me, stud?"

The man stubbornly kept quiet. Playing hard to get. Her crotch practically exploded with excitement.

"So you never said how they caught you."

More silence.

It didn't deter her. Just because he'd disappeared into his dark corner didn't mean she'd let him mope. Let him bask in the ray of sunshine that was her personality. Now that she'd drawn him into her orbit—the one where everything revolved around her—he would soon snap out of his funk and return to his evil overlord self.

"Ooh, is this a guessing game? I'll start. You got captured after a mighty battle fending off dozens of wyverns single-handedly until they overwhelmed you with sheer numbers."

He didn't reply.

"They sent a doppelganger, wearing my adorable face, meant to fool you into trusting her so that she could get close enough to drug you."

A snort from the shadows. "I never said you were adorable."

"You didn't have to." It went without saying. And lo and behold, he'd replied. "You must have marched valiantly into captivity in order to spare me from the wrath of this Suzie person."

"You seem to have me mistaken for someone noble. In my world, it's all about me."

It used *to be all about you. You'll soon learn, stud, just whom you exist for.*

"I'm running out of options. What does that leave? Ooh, I've got it. Your brother, Remiel, overcome with emotion at your reunification was also perturbed by your existence, and since he could not kill you, he handed you over to Suzie so he didn't have to get his hands dirty."

Another snort. "Remiel would have killed me himself given a chance. Alas for him, he never got one."

"Aliens descended—"

He interrupted. "It was my own stupidity that led me here. I was angry and upset after Sue-Ellen—"

Cough. "Hussy." Cough.

"—chose my brother."

"No need for that pale imitation of a dragon. You've got the real thing here, stud muffin." She skimmed her hands over her curves and, while she couldn't see his face, imagined he avidly stared. She would if the roles were reversed.

"Do you want to hear what happened or not?"

"Carry on." She gave an imperious wave.

He sighed. "As I said, I was pissed and wanted back what my brother stole from me—"

"Which, according to what I heard, you took from him." Such a delightful man, taking from others to enrich himself. Deka lived by the same rule. And look at that. They were both so misunderstood because of it.

He growled, a low, rumbly sound that almost had her tearing off her clothes and shouting, "Take me."

"Save the growling for later. I want to hear the rest."

"The rest involves me getting a phone call saying I had allies in Europe and instructing me to meet some people at an airfield so they could smuggle me out of the country. Like an idiot, I believed them. I even got in the box on my own, inhaled the gas, figuring a nap would be nice. When I woke, I found myself here, a prisoner of my own stupidity."

"It was a plausible story. There are factions within the Septs that would support your claim to the throne."

"Is the Silver Sept one of them?"

She snickered. "Not the North American branch. As if Auntie Zahra would follow anything less than full-blooded Golden. Even if Remiel were to disappear, she'd support her daughter's husband first."

"You speak of Brandon, the swamp gator? He was created in a lab." No mistaking the sneer in his tone.

"Yeah, but he's family. You're not." Yet.

"You're right. I have no family because I fucked it over. I gambled and lost." Such a defeated reply. It belonged to anyone but her evil overlord.

"Why haven't you escaped?"

"Why? Are you fucking kidding me?" That drew him from the shadows, an angry naked man stalking to the bars so that he might glare at her. "Do you think I haven't tried? I burned my hands to the bone trying to yank these bars apart." He held his palms up and showed her the traces of scars. "Every time that fat fucking jailer opened my cell, I tried to overpower him and escape."

"Don't tell me Jabba is stronger than a Golden dragon."

"Of course, not," he snorted with clear disdain. "But he has access to potions that knock me on my ass. Then he slaps on the cuffs, and I'm no better than a puny human."

"I don't know how they can live with themselves being so weak," she said, nodding in agreement.

"The weakness makes it impossible to escape, and each attempt results in punishment."

"Punishment is fleeting. Think of the agony you will deliver to your enemies when you escape."

"The punishment fucking hurts, and thoughts of vengeance don't do shit when your mind is being flayed from the inside."

Despite his earlier reluctance to speak, he now proved a fount of information. "Who is holding us captive? Who dares to invoke the wrath of the Silver Sept? We shall strip the skin from his flesh. Eat his organs one by one as he silently screams." Because a proper torture started with the tongue and ended with the eyes when there was nothing left to see.

"First off, it's a she, not a he. The suzerain is a female, but I'm not sure of what race. She is powerful, though, more powerful than you can imagine."

"Is she the same person who was screwing with the Crimson Sept?" The imposter had taken over the high priestess's body and caused all kinds of havoc. The shame of it would keep the Crimsons at the lower echelons of power for decades to come.

"She has the ability to take on any appearance she wishes. Even the one she shows me is probably not her true visage."

"Why does she want you?" She shook her head. "Never mind. Of course, she wants you. A virile Golden dragon in his prime and a contender for the throne."

"Fuck the throne. The damned thing has brought me nothing but trouble."

"Don't be so hasty." Because Deka really had her heart set on a crown. The heifers back home would be so jealous.

"I'm tired of all the politics and games. Ever since my birth, it's been 'Samael, do this.' 'Samael, say that.' Between Anastasia leading me around by the dick, and Parker with his goddamned experiments, I've yet to live my own life. To make my own choices. I'm tired of being a puppet to others."

"Then stop."

His gaze narrowed. "You say that like it's easy. As if I have a choice."

"Because you do. You're a dragon. And not just a dragon, a Golden one. No matter how you were born, or who the other half of you is, you belong to the most powerful line of dragons. You can literally do anything you want. And short of a full-scale war, there's nothing your brother, or even the Septs, can do."

"Maybe, once upon a time, I could have, but now…" His shoulders slumped. "I am nothing."

Before she could slap that morose expression from his face with words, the ceiling overhead rumbled. She peered upward and managed to say, "What the hell?" before water gushed from the ceiling, tons of it pouring out of tiny holes perforated overhead. She sputtered under the torrential downpour, skin soaked, garments sodden, her hair, already suffering from a kidnapping and bar hopping, a soggy mess.

It lasted long enough to cleanse every pore she had, and a few she was sure just appeared for the rainfall.

When it was done, stopping as suddenly as it had started, she glared at the ceiling. "That was rude."

"That was a sign."

"You mean that's happened before?" she asked, noting how nice his skin looked when slick.

"Not often, but when it does, it only means one thing."

"And that thing would be that Suzie wants us to drown? Grow gills?"

A grim expression pulled his features taut. "It means the suzerain wants me clean."

"Well, that's nice of her to care for her prisoners like that, but couldn't she install a shower? Maybe heat the water a little."

"She doesn't care about our comfort. She only bathes me because of what she wants."

"And what does she want?" Deka asked.

He didn't reply, and in the silence she heard their jailor approach, keys jingling at his waist, a slow, haunting whistle at his blubbery lips.

"Nothing." Samael stared downward, shoulders hunched. A shadow of the brash man she once knew.

"Surely, it can't be that bad." He didn't look too abused unless one counted the fact that he'd lost weight. He bore no fresh scars other than on his hands. Had all his limbs.

"There are things worse than death," he claimed, holding out his hands to their jailor, sliding both of them through a single set of bars so that Jabba might lock the special wristbands around them.

"What does she want from you?" she asked again as Jabba entered the cell and unlatched the collar at his neck.

Not answering, Samael meekly exited his cell and began a slow, plodding walk in front of their jailor. She could almost feel the shame rolling off him in waves.

"Where are you taking him? What does Suzie want?"

Jabba had no compunction and told her. More like he hummed it, and it was only after they were gone, as Deka repeated the familiar refrain to herself that she grasped the title of the tune.

Why is he singing, Just a Gigolo?

Then the light bulb went off.

"That bitch!" Suzie was pimping out her man.

Chapter Five

Marching up the hall, a cool draft brushed past Samael's dick. It swung as he walked, and in his old life he might have felt some embarrassment at his nudity. It didn't take long in here before he'd overcome that particular emotion. He'd not had any clothes since his arrival. Part of the breaking down of who he was. Who he used to be.

I was almost a king.

Now, as his jailor liked to remind him, he was a gigolo. Or would be if he'd give in to the suzerain's demands.

Fuck her if she thinks I'm giving her anything. He might not have much left. No home. No freedom. No power. But the sperm in his sac belonged to him!

I'll choose who gets it.

For now, at least. Until the suzerain tired of his refusal and took it by force. Just like she'd taken other things without permission.

The journey from the dungeon to the upper levels of the castle proved interesting. The stone work intricate and vast. The halls long and winding. The windows few and far between. Not that he saw much through them. The drapery kept them covered.

As a man who enjoyed an extensive nightlife, he never thought he'd miss the hot kiss of sunlight.

But he did, and he missed real food and his

bed and playing Stickman Golf on his phone. So many things he took for granted. So many things he'd never done or achieved.

So much pussy he'd never dipped his dick into.

I would have liked a taste of Deka's. The woman might only have gotten a cursory glance from him before, but mostly because he was otherwise preoccupied.

Now, however, with her residing in the cell across from him, he couldn't help but notice her.

Want her.

She would look lovely draped in jewels. His hidden hoard had more than enough to cover her body. Even better, he could imagine her splayed upon his heap of precious stones. Unlike a fragile-skinned human, he'd wager she wouldn't whine if the gems bit into her skin as he pounded into her sweet flesh.

And she would fuck him. The damned crazy woman said she'd come for him.

Why?

She made it sound as if she were interested in him as a man. As a lover.

She'd soon change her mind. Who'd want a broken thing like him?

Some days, when he opened his eyes, he cursed the fact that he'd woken, because the hopelessness weighed him down. Even the voice in his head, the one he'd listened to most of his life, had given up fighting.

He'd come to grips with his nightmare. Or thought he had. Her arrival, though, had him feeling off balance. Hope tried to break out of its cage. His arrogance simmered at the edges of the moat he'd surrounded it with.

This place didn't allow for either, and should the suzerain even guess he was ready to fight, the hammer would come down—and he didn't want Deka to hear him scream.

The jailor—that he tried not to think of as Jabba like Deka named him—stopped in front of a pair of regal doors. The black metal had been beaten into panels carved with intricate swirls. Despite Jabba not raising a fist to knock, they swung open at their approach, the lack of creaking more ominous than the cavernous room they opened to.

"Go in. The suzerain awaits. And you know she hates tardiness."

He knew, and a tiny part of him screamed, *Don't make her wait.*

Another part of him thought he should go find the kitchen and make himself a sandwich.

He stepped inside, and though the temperature didn't drop, his balls shrank, practically crawled back up inside his body.

Good thing Deka wasn't here. She wouldn't be so impressed with him now.

Nothing much had changed since his last visit. Still a ginormous space with an arching, ribbed ceiling, and pillars holding it up over a polished stone floor. All in black with striations of red.

The epitome of an evil throne room.

If it didn't evoke such painful memories, he'd covet it.

The room had a stark opulence to it. There wasn't much in the way of decoration or furniture—no paintings of ugly heirs, or spindly-legged antiques. The few pieces scattered in the vast room were expensive and decadent.

Take the super-sized throne, built out of the

skull of some massive beast—*say it, you know what it is.*

Fine. It was the skull of a dragon with spiraling horns inset within it, framing it on the sides. The white of the bone was covered in dark gems, not exactly rubies, although he'd seen the heart of them pulse with red fire.

Other than the throne, there was a fireplace, a massive open hearth that he'd yet to see filled with any flames. A shame. The cold room could have used some warmth.

The chain hanging from the ceiling was comprised of the dull metal that inhibited his dragon side, the dangling cuffs lined with velvet. The suzerain wanted to be the cause of his screams, not the metal.

He preferred the throne room visits to those of the bedroom with its massive four-poster bed, though. Some instinct for preservation wanted to keep him out of the mad woman's boudoir. A female he'd seen, yet knew for a fact wasn't the true face behind the illusion.

Could I handle seeing the truth?

Would she have tentacles? He hated tentacles. Nasty, wiggly things.

The air in the room changed, charged with a malevolent chill that pimpled his skin.

I am not afraid.

You should be.

The cowardly voice he'd acquired since his incarceration advised him to stand down. To behave, lest he incur punishment. There were times he wanted to ignore its sage advice. To rant and rail and fight.

Don't fight. You know what happens when you do.

Yeah, he felt like a man. As if he did something rather than accept his fate.

This is my life now. I can't change it.

Can't or won't?

As the chilly air was displaced by the approach of the suzerain, he didn't fidget.

He didn't run.

He didn't even turn his head to look or give a disparaging glance.

He wanted to. How he wanted to laser that bitch with his stare. To cow her with a sneer.

Don't fight. Obey.

The soft words in his head drew a sigh.

"Arms up."

Disobeying wasn't an option.

He raised his hands over his head, knowing the drill.

Magic pulled at the metal cuffs on his wrists, reeling them even higher overhead until he stood on tiptoe. The chain only jangled lightly as it clipped onto the eyelet hooks.

The position stretched his body tautly. Exposed him. Then again, he'd long ago lost anything to hide.

He stared straight ahead, and not just because he knew better than to turn. He didn't want to see. Perhaps if he pretended the suzerain didn't exist, then he could go back to his cell and that distracting temptation across from him.

The soft whisper of fabric on the stone floor let him know without peeking that she approached. His body held itself taut, a bowstring pulled tightly, ready to twang with release.

"There's my pet."

He didn't reply.

"I hear you've made friends with the new prisoner."

I have no friends.

Or family.

Probably because he'd screwed them all over.

"I wouldn't get too attached to her." The lilting voice had a husky undertone to it. "I have plans for her."

"She's a Silvergrace. Her disappearance won't go unnoticed."

"I should hope not. I am hoping for some pure panic on their parts as they run around like dragons with their tails cut off."

"Why?"

"Because it amuses me."

"What's the point of all this?" For the first time in a while, he found himself questioning. Wondering at the suzerain's purpose. She had power. Why these stupid games?

"Are you looking for a reason why I hate the dragons? Why I hate all of those you call cryptozoids? Do I need one?"

"Uh, yeah." He'd had one. He'd been jealous of his full-blooded Golden brother, so jealous that he wanted to take his place.

"If you knew my story, you'd understand why I do this. Why I taunt and tease. After all, where's the fun in killing? Once they're all dead, then who will amuse me?"

"You sent humans after the Silver Sept." He'd been there for that short, bloody battle.

"Expendable creatures. Not as fun or valuable as dragons. The mighty drakes, rulers of the skies and seas. Once also keepers of magic until one of them betrayed them all."

"How do you know all this?" Even Anastasia, as the Golden priestess, only had chunks of their past. Yet the suzerain spoke as if…as if she'd lived through it.

Impossible.

Is it? There were many things about this woman that made no sense.

Such as her capture and torture of him.

She took something of him each time they met. Not his seed, though. She never touched him.

Not once.

Good thing. His dick might never come out of hiding again.

But he wondered at times if what she did was worse.

She swayed closer, the tingle of her magic rippling over his skin. He fought not to flinch as she crept closer and spoke. "I am the keeper of the lore. The last bastion of true magic. The only one left of those locked away. As if they could keep us prisoner forever."

"Us?" This was the first time she'd alluded to someone else.

"A misnomer. And you are awfully inquisitive today. A good thing I find myself in a mellow mood. But don't test it."

Sharp pain jabbed at his skull, and he writhed, jaw open wide in a rictus, the scream caught in his lungs.

As quickly as it had begun, the pain ended, and he sagged in his bonds, letting the chain hold his weight.

It never got any easier.

"On to your purpose. Have you replenished enough to give me what I need?"

"Fuck you."

The slap cracked loudly across the skin of his cheek. It didn't really hurt, and didn't even move his head. Having suffered worse, it proved easy to stare straight ahead.

"Dragons. Always so stubborn. You continue to hurt yourself when it would be so much easier to give in."

Giving in would hurt less. When he stood still, he truly got to view the horror of watching his soul being sucked from his body. "I'll never give in." The words came out with a bit of force.

"Someone is a little feisty today." The laughter emerged low and chilling. "Show a little respect. We both know I could send you to your knees, begging me to kill you, with but a twitch of my hand."

"Why not just kill me?" He didn't want to feed this creature, and yet, he wasn't given a choice. Even now, his tattered soul had barely recovered from the last leeching.

The figure in the dark cloak moved in front of him, the wispy curls of the fabric dancing in an invisible breeze. "Kill you? But we're not done. However, you aren't quite ripe for the picking. We'll have to let you rest up a little longer. Which is why we picked up a spare."

"Spare what?"

"Your new dungeon companion, of course. A Silver dragon. So much tastier than those Reds I played with."

The thought of Deka suffering at the suzerain's hands roused an anger in Samael he'd thought doused. "Don't you dare hurt her."

"Or else what?" The cloak swirled against his skin, causing him to shiver as his skin contracted from the icy touch. The suzerain moved around him. "Will you promise to obey me and not fight if I leave her alone?"

Obey this foul creature to save a stranger?

Who is she but a girl who thinks you're more special than you are?

You are nothing.

Nothing but a traitor to my own kind.

Yet he could redeem himself. It would start with one act. One moment of bravery and heroism.

He looked at the cloaked figure, saw within the deep cowl the red, glowing eyes. The alien gaze that stirred something dark and frightening within.

The world will burn if she gets what she wants. Lovely, dancing flames. And screams. So many screams.

Surely, he didn't want that.

Give in, it's easier.

But on this, he wouldn't listen to the voice.

He dropped his head. "I don't care what you do to the woman. She means nothing." She only served as a reminder of the things he could no longer have.

"You heard the man. Take him back to his cell," the suzerain ordered. "And fetch me the girl."

A voice inside him, not the one that advocated he roll over and bare his belly, screamed, *Don't let her do this. You can save her. You can do it.*

No, I can't.

In this dark place, he didn't hold the title of king. He could barely call himself a man.

He was nothing but a coward.

Chapter Six

"What do you mean, she's in the bathroom again?" Aunt Xylia—who did not find it funny at all when her nieces giggled and called her Xylophone—asked as she called for the third time that day.

"She's got the runs. Bad. Must have been a bad baguette." Babette cringed even as the words came out of her mouth.

"Put her on the phone, right this instant."

"But—" Babette tried to think of another excuse to stall. Auntie saw right through it.

"Now!" When Aunt Xylia used that tone, you didn't argue, unless you had your affairs in order. Babette wondered if the paper napkin she'd written on when she turned eighteen counted.

I, Babette Silvergrace, of questionably sound mind, do hereby leave my hoard of marbles and organic seeds—totally untouched by GMOs—to my favorite cousin, Deka. But only if she avenges my death.

To which Deka, overwhelmed, had solemnly sworn with her hand over her heart to destroy whatever killed Babette. If it were a car crash, she'd have the car crushed and melted. Cancer? She'd damned well find a cure.

Because that was what best friends did! BFFs covered for each other unless Aunt Xylia was breathing through the phone, menacing Babette with bodily harm—which, given her access to potions, could get pretty hairy—then a girl spilled the beans.

"I don't know where she is right now."

"Is she with a man?" Auntie sounded cautiously hopeful.

"Kind of." At least, that was the plan. If Deka got caught by the right sort, then she was with Samael.

"Well, if she's off fornicating, then I guess that's all right. She did make them sign the contract first, didn't she?" Aunt Xylia's asked.

"Um, no, probably not. But don't worry, he's not human."

"Really?" Auntie's tone perked up. "Good for her. About time she forgot about that misfit D'Ore boy."

"Uh-huh." Babette hummed an agreement, hoping to hide the lie.

Auntie zeroed in on it. "Tell me she's not with Samael."

"Well, um, see, that is, I don't know for sure if she is or not."

"Where is she?"

"A direct question. How to dodge it? "I don't know."

"Don't you dare cover for her. Tell me where my daughter is."

"I can't because I haven't heard from her since last night." The last text at one a.m. local time said simply, *Grabbed some free condoms to do water balloons. See you in a few.*

Deka always knew how to have fun, and a balcony attached to their room had so many possibilities.

Except Deka never came back to their room.

And while Babette wouldn't admit it aloud, she was kind of glad Auntie had called, freaking out.

Auntie's voice emerged low and clipped. "You mean to tell me your cousin went missing last night. Her phone is untraceable, and you're only thinking to tell me now?"

"I would have waited longer, but you kind of pushed the issue." Deka would be pissed Babette hadn't covered for long enough.

"I knew it was a bad idea to send you overseas. I'll be on the next plane."

"We don't know that she's in trouble."

The silence proved palpable. Mostly because of the inanity of her statement.

Babette sighed. "Let me know when your flight comes in. I'll meet you."

She hung up and groaned. A slender hand trailed over her bare arm, and a husky voice whispered, "How long before you have to meet your aunt?"

"Long enough to make you feel like a woman," she said with a grin before diving on her new lover.

Imagine the luck of running into Suzanne in the hall their first week here on her way to get ice. Now, if only the woman didn't have to keep running off to take care of business. Apparently, she was caring for some animals that required close supervision.

Speaking of which. "While I'd love to stay, I have to go." The lithe body rose from the bed, Suzanne's shape pure perfection. Her skin, mahogany excellence. Her hair curly to the extreme.

And while the occasional red spark in her brown-eyed depths seemed cause for concern, one kiss from those ruby lips and Babette forgot everything. Even the fact that she was worried about Deka missing.

I'm sure Deka's fine.

Chapter Seven

Having a fine time. Not.

Of Samael, she'd yet to see anything since he'd left. *Found him and lost him.*

In the meantime, Deka was so bored. Those simple words were enough back home to get her tossed out of the mansion and told to run off some energy.

I need to do something, or I am gonna snap.

Thankfully, Jabba's ugly twin brother, who bore a wisp of hair on top of his head but no teeth, came to fetch her.

Jabba Two jangled the cuffs in front of the bars and lisped, "Give me your hands."

"And if I don't?" she asked, tucking them behind her back.

"Then I use this." He held up a bag. Not a very interesting bag.

"Is this like a bean bag toss game? Are you going to lob it at me and knock me out?"

"The powder inside will put you to sleep. I'd like that." He leered and licked his blubbery lips.

While not her type, Jabba Two at least recognized her hotness; he just didn't have permission to touch it.

Her nose tilted. "There are laws against that kind of thing."

"Human laws don't apply here."

"My boyfriend is the jealous type. He'll totally kick your ass if you touch me." And she knew this because she would totally rip the eyes out of any woman's head that dared the same. Then she'd tear off their arms and whack them. Or should she leave the eyes intact so they could see their own fists coming in for a slap?

The choices.

"Ahem. Your hands."

How rude, interrupting her mental replay of the best way to avenge herself if jealous. "What if I don't want to go visit your boss? Did it occur to you that I might be busy? Tell her to make an appointment."

The big Jabba brother stared at her, slack-jawed. Put in his place for his impertinent behavior.

"You have to obey," he exclaimed.

"Or what? I'm already enjoying the hospitality of your dungeon cell. You've ruined my hair. And since you took my purse, I can't even fix my makeup."

"The suzerain will flail you for your disobedience."

"The suzerain needs to learn that the world doesn't revolve around her. And on the topic of your boss, who is she?"

"Not someone to be trifled with."

"Neither am I."

"Says the woman in a cage."

Hold on a second, did this doofus seriously just disparage her? "I am here by choice."

"Sure, you are. You can't get out."

"I could so, if I wanted to."

The smirk on his face claimed otherwise.

She sighed and stuck her hands through the bars.

"That's a good girl. Maybe she won't punish you too hard." Jabba clipped the manacles around her wrists, and she yanked them back through then held an impatient foot still as he turned the key in the three sets of locks.

The door opened, and she stepped out before declaring, "I told you I could get out of this cage."

He blinked. Probably in awe of her escape skills.

"But you're my prisoner." He pointed to the handcuffs.

She shook them and smiled. "Am I, Jabba Two? Or am I just letting you think I am?"

Poor man couldn't follow her elegant logic. The line of drool probably a sign his brain was melting from her sheer greatness.

"Take me to your leader," she declared with a toss of her head.

"Smirk while you can," grumbled her second jailor. "You'll be sobbing by the time she's done with you."

"You don't know me very well if you think I'd cry." Her lips curled into a smile that Babette had declared positively demonic. "Making people cry, though…" She bared some teeth. "I'm very good at that."

The corpulent male, his size massive, was covered in a loose robe, the brown fabric coarse, and she wasn't quite sure he walked on the floor so much as he slithered.

There was something oddly fascinating and, at the same time, horrifying about his appearance. *Because there is something familiar about him.*

Yet also perverted and grotesque. He made her skin crawl and her psychotic side—the one her mother told her to never bring out to play—twitch in agitation.

Not good. Whenever she let that twitch take over, listened to that sibilant whisper—*Let me out!*—it always led to mayhem.

Good times.

Forbidden times, she reminded herself.

Expensive, call-the-lawyers kinds of times.

Still…

If it were an emergency, surely mother would understand.

Mother maybe, Aunt Zahra? Tight-fisted boss lady had this thing about paying damages and the family reputation. She might actually cut Deka off one day, which was the only reason Deka didn't unleash and kill Jabba Two.

More surprising than her restraint, though, was the fact that his stench didn't make all her systems croak.

Apparently, he didn't indulge in bathing like she and Samael were forced to.

Talk about being at a disadvantage. She peeked down at her dress and grimaced. How to improve upon the damp fabric and her scraggly hair?

She quickly improvised, asking questions as she ripped at her dress and tore off strips.

"How long have you been working for Suzie?" Deka asked.

"Who? I work for the suzerain and no one else."

"Duh. I got that. For how long, though?" Really, did nobody understand things nowadays?

They're doing it on purpose to be stupid, Mother. They

really could use a slap. Can I give them one? Please.

A lack of an actual reply probably meant no.

Or is that yes… The walls could use some color.

"I've been with the suzerain since before the Roman Empire fell."

"You're like ancient," she replied with a wrinkle of her nose. Her hands deftly adjusted her new midriff-baring top, tethered between her cleavage with a strip of cloth to give it a halter-top appearance. "Did you always look like one of those things cook picks out of our garden and then cooks in garlic butter?" Those plump snails also looked rather ugly when popped from their shells but tasted delicious once roasted.

Hmm. She eyeballed him.

Jabba Two didn't notice. It was almost offensive.

"I didn't always look like this." The tone had a definite sadness to it. "But appearances don't matter. I lived while others didn't."

"Others? You mean there were more like you?" And what exactly did that mean? Jabba Two and his brother certainly weren't like anything she'd ever seen before.

Never even heard of, and her mother had taught her quite a bit about the world that existed beneath the human one.

"The exiled were few and yet many when forced to live apart. Over time, not all survived, and without outsiders to swell our ranks, our numbers dwindled."

She finished tugging at her skirt and eyed him with curiosity. "Didn't you have babies?" The first thing any species should do if faced with extinction was procreate. The dragons survived the human culling only because of strict breeding protocols.

They had to be careful because, without a Golden king to give them a helping nudge, dragons could only make dragons with each other. Humans, the most common other mate, produced sterile wyverns.

Not anymore. If Remiel began to bless those unions, then soon, the world would swim in dragons.

And then true hoarding and mayhem would begin.

Samael would be a part of that chaos. Anyone could see a wicked—ly sexy—ruler hid in that body. She planned to draw it out.

Jabba Two spoke lowly. "Infertility was a problem. Even longevity." He stopped in front of a wooden door carved with flowers. "Until we discovered a dark path."

"A dark path to where?" she asked. Discovering new places was her lady-boner moment. Some guys used cars. Some gals had shoes. Deka poked her nose in places she shouldn't.

"It led us all into damnation." The door swung open at his touch.

Given Jabba Two didn't enter, she handed him the scraps left over from her dress as a tip. Kind of like the royal court used to give tokens to their champions.

Ye are my champion of smell.

Also information. A picture formed, one piece at least. As she discovered more parts, maybe she'd understand.

"This is nice," she said with admiration as she entered the room. The halls she'd come through might have been plain; however, the lavish bedroom showed some comforts.

Plush white carpeting that her toes sank into. A marble fireplace, gleaming brightly with silver flames dancing in it. A divan, the single armrest displaying a furry gray pillow.

The *pièce de résistance* was the bed, a monstrous four-poster thing piled high with a mattress and pillows, the silver-stitched comforter plush and inviting.

"About time you upgraded my accommodations." Deka fluffed her hair, which she'd bound into a messy bun atop her head.

"These are the suzerain's quarters."

"You mean Suzie is letting me have her room?" She clasped her hands. "Best evil kidnapper evah!"

"What? No. You misunderstand."

She waved off Jabba Two as she entered the room. The table by the divan held a tray.

"Oooh. Snacks. But I don't see any wine. Fetch a bottle from the cellar."

"This isn't for you. You are to stand here and wait for—"

Holding a half-eaten piece of cheese in front of her mouth, she interrupted him. "Yeah, you can stop talking now. I wait for no one, except our matriarch. Oh, and my mother." Her brow furrowed. "And I guess my king, too. But that's it, unless they're super important."

"I am more important than you."

Despite his blobby face, he managed an indignant expression, and his complexion turned a rather interesting shade of orange. Once he reached red, would he be like a lobster, all done?

The piece of cheese didn't survive. Nom nom. Another piece followed it while Jabba Two had a mini fit.

Since Aunt Yolanda taught them to ignore those beneath them, she kept nibbling. But, eventually, she couldn't help herself. "Where's the wine? I tried to let you have your moment there, but it's interrupting my drinking time. Fetch it before I complain to Suzie about her lazy staff. Mother always says you gotta watch them like hawks. Except we can't eat them if they're slow."

"I am not your servant," he spat before walking—slithering?—away.

Deka sat in a chair and nibbled some more, the grapes providing some sustenance.

Could have really used some wine, though. Hopefully, Jabba would hurry back with it.

"Who told you to sit?" The voice came from behind her.

Interesting as she'd not heard anyone approach. "You may join me," Deka offered quite graciously. Aunt Yolanda would be so proud.

"Your temerity is rather fascinating."

"Your attempt at sounding tough isn't." Deka hid a yawn behind a hand, remembering her manners.

"You think this is a joke?"

She leaned back in her seat, but still didn't crane to look.

Never give them an advantage. She could practically hear Aunt Waida in her ear. *When you can, always assume a position of power.*

Which, in many cases, meant making them come to you.

A swirl of smoky fabric drifted into her line of sight. It billowed in alternating directions without a breeze.

The strange, wispy cloak covered a slender

frame that stood taller than she, but one not likely heavier.

The deep hood hid the face. Poor thing must be hideous. It brought out the compassion in Deka. "I know a good plastic surgeon if you need help."

"Help? I don't need help," the feminine voice hissed.

"If you say so. I've got a guy who can get you paper bags if you'd like a break from the hood."

"I don't hide because of my face."

"Says you. I'm going to assume you're butt ugly."

The slender fingers tugged back the hood, revealing fine features, a long, straight nose, full lips, and eyes that shone red.

Deka canted her head. "I don't suppose you're related to Rudolph."

"Insolence," Suzie yelled, those bright irises flaring.

Deka made a note: *might be working for Santa.* Good to know. She could use an in for some cool high-tech stuff.

"So, now that I've got you here, I need to file a complaint. A few actually. One, where is my luggage? I assume when your staff came to find me as a guest that they thought to bring along my things."

Suzie blinked. She could have really used some mascara for those short lashes. It would totally make those red suckers pop.

"And where's the wine? I am thirsty, dude. If you're going to offer cheese and grapes, the wine"— she pointed to the almost empty tray—"needs to be imbibed with it."

"That wasn't for you."

"Well, that's rude. Here I am, letting you bask

in my presence, and you can't even provide an adequate snack. You suck at being a hostess. If you'd like, I can have Aunt Yolanda refer you to an etiquette instructor. You know, so you don't faux pas." Look at that. More French. Perhaps this second language thing wasn't so hard after all.

"Enough."

The word rang out with vibration, the two syllables striking her skin and freezing her. Holding her immobile.

The woman in the robe moved closer and crouched down. Staring into the red holes of the woman's eyes, Deka noticed a swirling in them. An eternal loop, around and around.

Pretty.

"Answer me."

"Sorry, were you talking?" Deka asked.

Suzie's lips pursed. "How is it your impertinence keeps growing?"

"Mother says it's a gift." She smiled. "I'm also able to burp the alphabet, but I'm not supposed to brag about that one in public."

"Who sent you?"

"Do you really think I take orders from anyone?" She sometimes took suggestions that paid off, but mostly Deka just wandered at will.

"I captured you, which means you've failed as a spy."

"Failure is such a harsh word. And did it ever occur to you I just arrived?" She smiled. "You've yet to see what I can do."

"Your optimism is going to be lovely to crush."

"I am going to miss you when you're gone." As Deka carried on a conversation, she pushed at the compulsion holding her. It wasn't the first time someone had tied her up—and failed to hold her. She wondered if the father she never knew had a touch of Houdini in him.

"Tell me why you were searching for Samael." Suzie stood and paced, the robe snapping in a stiff breeze with her agitation.

"I thought Sammy skipped out on me. Which is totally uncool, especially considering the universe has made him my mate."

That got Suzie to whip around. "Samael is unclaimed."

"Because you stole him before I could take him." There was no doubt the man would want her. *It's fate.*

"Samael isn't for you."

"Holy shit." Understanding widened her eyes. "I get why you don't want me to get with him. You have a crush on me." She leaned forward, total compassion in her tone. "It's okay. It happens a lot on account I'm so incredibly awesome and sexy. It's a wonder anyone can move on after they've met me. Everyone else pales in comparison. But you'll have to get over me because I belong to Samael."

"I have no interest in you like that."

"You keep telling yourself that. I'm sure in time you'll believe it."

Teeth gritted, and those eyes took on a strobing pulse. "Your insistence on Samael belonging to you is laughable. He barely knows you exist."

Deka waved a hand. "Details. And again, your fault. You interrupted the natural progression of our courtship."

"There will be no courtship. No mating with him either. Because you'll be joining with me."

"With you?" Deka tilted her head and pursed her lips. "Hate to break it to you, darling, but I don't swing that way. I prefer some sausage for my bun, if you get what I mean."

"Indeed, I do," Suzie said, whirling enough to present her back. "I have to say," she continued in a now low-timbered voice, "that I prefer to fuck rather than be fucked. The term driving you like a hammer comes to mind."

The transformation proved so fluid that Deka had to blink to realize it had happened. But when she did... "Holy shit, you're a hermie."

"A what?" Said in a deep, masculine rumble.

"Hermaphrodite. You know, a person with guy and gal equipment. Totally, awesomely cool, which leads me to wonder, why do you need a boyfriend or girlfriend at all? I mean, aren't you your own best friend? I'd rather date my BFF, which, in your case, means you could fuck yourself." Her toned turned to hero-worshipping adoration. "It would be like the ultimate masturbation. Hot damn, you should get your own live feed channel. You could make a fortune doing it to yourself for a crowd."

The man, tall and tanned, much broader of shoulder now and possessed of ruggedly handsome features stared at her.

Being stared at in awe by people was kind of powerfully cool. She smiled, accepted it graciously, but at the same time that fact that she stole people's breath away made for one-sided conversations.

"You know you can speak to me," Deka advised. "Don't be shy. I know it can be intimidating meeting someone like me for the first time."

"You seem to think you're in control of the situation, and yet I"—an invisible hand clasped her by the hair and lifted her—"am the one actually holding the power."

Having had her hair forcibly yanked and pulled growing up—and every time she got in a fight with any of her cousins since—Deka didn't really react much. She dangled a few inches off the floor with her arms crossed.

"This is why you need etiquette lessons. This is not acceptable host behavior."

The face leaned close to hers to hiss, "You will listen to me."

Her nose wrinkled. "How about instead you find some mouthwash because Evil Kidnapper breath is preventable. And so is gingivitis."

He flung her, and because she'd had plenty of practice, she landed on her feet.

Slowly, she turned, tucking stray hairs behind her ears. Smiled at him, making note of his sneer, then rushed him, headfirst. She made it two steps before he muttered, "Freeze."

She stopped moving, one leg up and bent, arms outstretched. Freeze dance taken to the extreme.

He walked over to her. "Now who's in charge, bitch?"

Through stiff lips, she managed to say, "Who's suffering from little dick syndrome?"

She expected the slap, and thus braced for it. Before a second blow could land, a knock sounded. While her Wattpad story would describe it as ominous and full of portent, in reality, it was a quick flurry of taps.

Suzie—or should she now call him Hermie?—yelled, "What is it?"

"There is a problem in the dungeon." The door opened, and the jailor entered. Slithered, rather.

"Short of it being swallowed by a rock worm, I highly doubt it's urgent," snapped Suzie.

"You need to come and deal with it."

"I'm not done with the girl."

"Play with her later. You need to handle the situation in the dungeon now." Jabba One—recognizable by his less nasally voice—insisted.

Suzie scowled. "I do not understand your urgency. The prisoner is in his cell, is he not?"

"Yes."

"And you put on his collar?"

"I did."

"Then what's the problem?"

Jabba rumbled, "The dragon is rampaging."

"And? He can't escape."

"That's just it." Jabba took a look at her and moved closer, lowering his voice.

Hello, she could still hear him just fine.

"He's snapped the chain and cracked the walls."

"What has him so agitated? I thought we'd finally broken him," said Suzie/Herm.

"It appears as if the woman is the trigger."

Ah, how cute. Samael was having a fit and, according to Jabba, a jealous one. She couldn't help but smile.

Two pairs of eyes swiveled to look at her. She managed a tiny wave from her awkward pose.

"Grab the girl. I want to test your theory."

How predictable. They were going to use her as bait.

She couldn't wait for Samael to take it—ahem, her.

Chapter Eight

Anger seethed in Samael, a formless, shapeless thing that pulsed as he paced his cell, the links of his chain rattling.

I should have done something.

It bothered him that he hadn't. The cowardly voice inside, the one that was now silent, had made it seem like the only choice.

But it was the wrong choice.

I should have done something to save her.

But you're weak. And stupid. And a coward.

Arrrrgh! He beat at his chest, a dark, roiling push of emotion bursting out of him, splitting skin and bone, reshaping him, the collar at his neck almost snapping as his serpentine one filled it.

He hated wearing his dragon in here. It seemed a travesty to make his greater self suffer. Yet the need in him was too great.

Arrrrrrruuu. The warbling trumpet of his discontent echoed in the cavernous room. The cell might prove more than sizeable for his human shape, but now he was large and light. All his flesh, an atomic latticework of bio matter, stretched thin, yet solid enough to provide decent armor against most attacks.

Why am I so weak?

He never used to be weak.

She's taken almost all my soul.

That doesn't explain all your actions.

When did he become craven?

Had he truly fallen that low? Even he should have some standards.

I should have saved her.

The thought reverberated inside, filling him with anxiety, making him pace; however, the sizeable chamber was not large enough for his fury. He kept pivoting too quickly. He rumbled toward one wall.

How dare it stand in my way?

Slam.

He barreled into it, the force causing a tremor. Stray drops of water from the shower earlier fell from the ceiling.

No escape.

He whirled and charged back in the other direction, running as fast as his dragon legs could go.

Wham.

Another brute force attack against the offending wall.

A dragon should not be caged.

He wailed at the injustice of it, a sharp, bright sound, before chugging back in the other direction, his chain rattling loosely behind, torn from the wall in his fury.

Over and over he charged. Hit. Failed to smash the turmoil amassing within.

By now she's probably got her arms pulled tautly, exposing that luscious body of hers.

My body!

Slam.

Is she being hurt? The pain meted out by the suzerain, not that of a whipping or beating. Physical pain could be handled, but the pain of someone shredding through your mind, tearing open every vulnerability, every secret… It hurt. Hurt so much. And then even worse was when the hurting stopped and pieces of you just disappeared.

I should have helped her.

He should have had some fucking balls. Should have acted. Then he wouldn't be stuck in a cell, collared like a beast, racing back and forth, slamming into walls, making the entire structure shake.

"Hey, stud muffin, miss me?"

The sudden bright appearance of her voice stalled him in his tracks. His large head swiveled, and he glanced through the bars to see Deka marching ahead of the jailor, her skin unmarred, her dress somehow different than before.

His gaze narrowed. She appeared too brave. She must be hiding the pain.

A swirl of darkness filled the corridor. The bloody suzerain, the one behind all his problems, stalked toward the cells, probably called upon because of Samael's behavior.

Good.

It'd worked.

If the suzerain were here, then she wasn't torturing Deka.

A low growl, one not heard in a while, rolled from him. His dragon shape shrank rapidly with a snap as Samael snarled, "Did that bitch hurt you?"

"As if, Sammy." Deka stopped in front of his cell and twirled. "Right as rain." She stopped, facing him. "Did you miss me?"

"Sammy?" The deep voice had a familiar hint, and yet…

Samael's head snapped as he turned to look at

the suzerain, only he noted the shape was different. Taller, broader, and the hands…

He grabbed the bars and pressed his face against them before asking, "Who are you?"

"Don't you recognize me," mocked the voice. It came from a man, one with dark hair raised in a crow's wing, but those eyes… Those red-iris eyes.

"It's you. It can't be." His forehead wrinkled.

"You didn't know about Hermie?" Deka said with a hint of surprise. "Half man, half woman. And, apparently, hasn't seen the possibilities in exploiting that for the masses."

"Your new cellmate is mouthy, *Sammy*." No mistaking the mockery. "I look forward to punishing it out of her."

His grip on the bars tightened. Metal groaned.

Deka looked suitably impressed. About time he did something along those lines. She drew close and reached out a finger to trace over the ones gripping the bars.

A jolt of something went through him. A sense of awareness that he knew she felt.

"How are you holding the bars?" she asked, a simple query that took him a moment to figure out because, in his mind, she'd said something more along the lines of: *Let me suck your dick.*

Oral was always the first thing on a guy's mind followed by, *Damn, her hand would look nice wrapped around my dick.* And finally, *She's pretty nice. I wonder if she wants a spin on my dick.*

"Are your bars defective?" She slid her hand away from him onto the metal. Sucked in a breath.

He knocked her hand away. "Don't do that."

Her head cocked. "How come you're not screaming?"

"Enough chatter. Put the Silver back in her cage."

The jailor moved in her direction, but Deka didn't wait for him. She walked into her cage, turned, and waved her hand at the suzerain. "Go. I'm done talking to you. If you stay, I shall ignore you. You are the worst host ever."

The trap she'd laid was lovely. Samael admired it to the point he had to drop his hands.

The suzerain was royally fucked. If he left, it seemed as if he obeyed her. If he stayed, which everyone knew he didn't mean to do, he also lost face.

The elegance was beautiful.

And the suzerain knew it. "You might think you've won for now, but you seem to forget, if you prove too difficult, I will get my hands on another."

If Deka kept irritating, the suzerain would leave Deka alone.

The next words ruined that hope.

"I don't need you, and it's been a while since we've roasted a dragon."

"Aunt Waida says we're best eaten slow-basted over a coal fire. You should get a rub, too, to match the color of the scales. For a Silver, you want to do a sea salt and pepper rub. The spices are rubbed under the scales. Some folks make the mistake of skinning first, yet they shouldn't because the skin acts as a foil baking the insides."

Samael wasn't the only one who took time to digest the fact that Deka seemed rather well acquainted with cooking dragons.

The jailor slammed the door shut, and the locks clicked.

Samael seethed at the bars, still gripping them, yet not burning. This wasn't the first time he'd managed it. Probably building immunity.

I'm just special.

"We'll see if you're still laughing when we skewer and roast you." The suzerain whipped around, his cloud cloak swirling with him, covering his retreat.

"About time you left. I swear some people just can't take a hint when they've overstayed their welcome," she remarked, loud enough for all to hear.

Jabba smirked as he scurried after the suzerain, leaving them alone.

How awkward.

I would have said romantic. The distinctly womanish voice came inside his head, but wasn't one he'd heard before.

Have I finally cracked and found my feminine side?

The laughter didn't help.

"Sammy," Deka called him. "Look at me, stud muffin."

He rotated his gaze to find hers. Her green gaze held fire in it, and he felt his own eyes glow in reply. Staring through the bars, a spark of something ignited in him. It burned the edges of the darkness inside.

It brought forth words he'd thought himself incapable of saying. "We are getting out of here."

She clasped her hands. "Are you getting impatient, too, stud muffin? I, for one, can't wait for your hands to worship my body."

Okay, he couldn't wait for that either, but that wasn't his primary reason for getting out of here.

Wait, why isn't it?

As his anger cooled, the metal he gripped heated.

"Fuck." He stepped away from the bars, and Deka uttered a, "Hmmm."

"What's that supposed to mean?" he asked.

"Just finding your reaction to the bars interesting. I was always taught no dragon could touch dracinore metal without suffering, and yet you did it for a while there."

"Delayed reaction."

"Could be, or it doesn't affect you like a pureblood."

He bristled and puffed his chest. "Are you implying I'm not a drake?" An alpha male dragon capable of ruling.

"You've got plenty of balls, stud. But I also know from my mommy's tests that you're not a pure Gold."

"Are you going to mock me for being a half-breed? That seems ironic given you're not pure Silver."

"I'm like three-quarters," she stated. "And no one's mocking anyone."

"Yet." The moment was still young. The possibilities endless.

"What I'm saying is, you're half something, but my mom couldn't figure out what. What if that half isn't affected by dracinore?"

"If that were true, why doesn't it work all the time?"

"A hybrid trait. It probably has to be triggered. What did the times you were immune have in common?"

"I was angry."

"Why were you angry this time, Sammy?" She stepped closer to the bars and trailed a finger down her cleavage to a knot.

"I don't like games."

"Only losers hate playing. And neither of us is

a loser, stud. I know you were jealous."

"Was not."

"You totally should be. Suzie is totally after my body."

"He touched you?" He couldn't help the shouted words.

"He wanted to. Alas, he was interrupted by my super jealous boyfriend."

"I am not your boyfriend." He was more than that.

I'm her mate.

The concept made him faint.

Chapter Nine

Poor Samael. The man was quite overcome, probably with worry about her.

She could tell he thought her a delicate flower in need of his protection. So sexy. But nothing wrong with showing him from time to time that she was strong. Soon, he'd get to see just how wonderful an assertive woman could be—especially in bed.

He won't need to sign a waiver.

Her libido rubbed its greedy hands in glee.

"Don't worry that pretty Gold head of yours. We'll soon be getting out of here."

"Have you finally lost what few marbles you had left?" was his sarcastic reply as he struggled from his face-plant position to a sitting one.

"Oh, please. I lost those a long time ago to cousin Mary. She collects the damned things. If you want to win at anything with her, just grab a bag from the dollar store and scatter them to distract her."

"Isn't that cheating?"

She blinked. "Your point being?"

A rusty chuckle emerged, and it was with a hint of wonder he mumbled, "Holy fuck, I never thought I'd find a reason to laugh again."

"This is just the beginning, stud muffin. You and I are going to have glorious adventures together, lots of laughter, and insanely hot sex."

"Sounds overly optimistic given our situation."

"A moment ago, you said we would escape."

"A moment ago, I temporarily forgot the situation. It's still shit, in case you hadn't noticed."

"Dungeon half full, stud. You gotta see the positive around you."

"What's positive about being held in a dragon-proof cell?"

"Well, for one thing, you're only half dragon. And two, I'm here." She flung out her hands and sang, "Ta-da!"

"I don't see how that helps."

"Because you're grumpy on account you're probably horny. Don't worry. We'll fix that real soon."

"You keep saying that, yet I've yet to hear your concrete plan to escape." He indicated the walls and bars of his prison cell. "I've tried. This place was made to resist a dragon."

She patted the stone wall. "It totally was. You've got to hand it to our European ancestors. They knew how to build dungeons. But, while they are great at keeping us from busting out, that doesn't stop someone from getting in."

"Who would come here?" He waved a hand at their surroundings. "There isn't even a Starbucks around."

"Don't say the S word," she moaned. "I could go for a hibiscus drink right about now," she muttered. "I'll be posting a less-than-stellar review about this castle on *TripAdvisor*. With a highlight on the lack of amenities." She shook her fist at the ceiling. "Would it kill you to have some coffee?"

"No one is coming to rescue us because no

one knows we're here."

"Don't be so sure of that. I found you."

"Yes, you found me. But let me ask you, did you tell anyone where you went? Do you even know where we are?"

She waved a hand. "Not yet. A minor detail that I will solve once I get a peek out of a window."

"Even if you did manage to look, and hell, let's say you saw an address, who would you tell? We have no phone. No internet. No fucking flares even." He ticked the items off on his fingers. "I hate to break it to you, spoiled princess, but no one is coming because no one knows where *this*"—big gesture to the space around them—"is."

"Correction, my Golden stud. They do know." She slapped her butt. "Mother had me chipped after the third time I went missing at the mall."

"Your mom chipped you like a dog?"

Her nose wrinkled. "Well, she didn't put it like that. Her exact words were, 'Precious darling Deka, I would be devastated and probably throw myself into an abyss should you ever come to any harm due to my parental negligence in watching over you.'"

"Your mother said that?" He didn't hide his skepticism.

"Not in those exact words, but that was the gist. I mean, how else would you translate 'Demon spawn, I'm going to put a tracker in you before child services tries to charge me with child abandonment?' Same thing."

"Totally."

She couldn't help but beam at him. "I knew you'd understand. My family doesn't always get me. Apparently, some shrink told my mom I had some dissociative disorder. She also claimed I had a dose of narcissism and a fancy word I can never pronounce."

"Mine told me I had a superiority complex," he shared.

Her nose wrinkled. "What's wrong with that?"

"That's what I said."

"Did your shrink know you were a Gold? Because I kind of think you're obliged to have a god complex given your genes."

"See, you understand, but would that prick listen?"

"No!" She clasped her hands eagerly. "So you ate him for his temerity."

"I wish. Anastasia wouldn't let me. So I returned that night and burned down the place." He paused. "While he was in there with his mistress." A smile crested his lips, and she returned it, excited by the peeking of his previous arrogance.

There's the dragon I want as a mate.

"Vengeance is yummier than anything. When we get out of here—" she said.

You're gonna get naked and bend over for me. She heard his thought as clear as day but didn't let it distract her.

"We're gonna—"

Come so hard on my cock, you'll choke on it.

Ooh, that almost made her veer off tangent, but she held strong and finished. "Get you some clothes."

"What?"

Why does she want to dress me?

She could hear and understand his confusion, given both their fantasies involved removing them.

She explained. "Yes, clothes, my naughty, naked stud. Once my crew arrives, it wouldn't do for them to ogle you. I like most of them and would hate to have to kill them."

"For staring."

"Exactly." She beamed. "I knew you'd understand. Which will make it easier to avoid any jealous psychotic episodes."

"You're jealous? Of me?"

"I know, surprising given that I usually outshine everything around me, but you are pretty nifty, and I can see some of the heifers thinking they could make a pass at you. Totally unacceptable, of course."

"Of course," he replied faintly. "Does this mean I am allowed to insist you wear turtlenecks?" *Lest anyone admire the smooth line of her neck.*

She heard the thought clearly. It brought a giddy feeling inside. "You might want to insist on baggy track pants. Just like you might have to endure ugly haircuts, the kind where I trim it with a bowl on your head."

His lips twitched. "Or we could both stun the world with our looks, let them ogle us, and, after a glorious jealous fight, have screaming make-up sex."

She sighed. "You say the sweetest things. All that's left to add is that right after the third orgasm you give me, I say we go grab a big fat cheeseburger, loaded with toppings, fries, and a milkshake because we need to get some meat back on those bones."

"The dungeon diet has left me a little skinnier than before." He peeked down at his frame.

"I don't mind a bit of bone, but only when it comes with a steak. Oh, and I'll make an exception for your cock."

Poor guy choked. Probably swallowed the wrong way.

"Don't worry, my hot stud. Soon you'll be

gasping for air because I'll be riding you like a cowgirl." Bareback. No point in waiting. Her biological clock was ticking, and she needed to catch up. A few cousins and friends had already popped out some cute babbling runts. She wanted to smell like baby powder and vomit, too.

He turned serious. "Do you really think sex should be high on our list? I mean the suzerain has evil plans. Shouldn't we be concerned about the fate of the world…?"

She stared at him.

"Possible extinction of mankind, famine, war…?"

She stared some more until he slowed and finished with. "You're right. Fuck 'em all. They can wait while I do you until your toes curl."

My toes have been curling from the first moment I met you.

She didn't say it aloud, yet she caught the widening of his eyes. The lines of communication between them were expanding. It was often the case with mated pairs, especially now that they'd touched and formed a light bond.

Sex would cement it.

While she waited for the heifers to raid the castle, they spent a while chatting. The old, brash Samael she'd glimpsed from before surfacing at first in bits and pieces, then longer stretches.

This was the man, the dragon, the almost king, she'd fallen for.

The evil glint he got in his eye, though, that was why she loved him.

"I might have a plan to get out of these cells," he claimed.

Given her girl parts had sucked all the blood

from her brain, making it impossible to think, she was glad he'd finally come up with something. Because Babette and the crew were taking their sweet time showing up.

Seriously. They should have been here by now. Perhaps the place was better guarded than it appeared. Just having seen Jabba One and Two didn't mean there weren't more guards or security devices.

Deka's personal hoard-hiding spot was something out of a *Tomb Raider* movie with hidden pits, fiery arrows, and poisonous darts. She even had a giant boulder that dropped.

Only problem was, it didn't just squish intruders; it smooshed her treasure, too.

Getting blood and gore out of flattened gold filigree was a bitch. At least she'd learned not to keep any action figures in that spot after the first loss. She still had yet to replace the Ewok village from the eighties.

"What's the plan, stud?"

"When our jailor comes with our next meal, seduce him."

"Um, as my super jealous boyfriend, shouldn't you be against that?"

His gaze fixed her. "Are you attracted to him?"

"Not particularly."

"And I never said you have to go very far. You need to get him close enough to steal his keys. Then toss them to me while you hold him off."

"You want me to fight him?" She pointed to herself. "How come this plan doesn't involve you seducing him and tossing me the keys while you overpower him?"

"It won't work." He shrugged. "I tried. I'm

not their type."

"You do realize, if I do this, it counts as me saving you."

"I'm sure we'll have an opportunity to even that score."

"Is everything going to be competition with you?" she asked, hand on her hip.

"Probably."

She smiled. "Soul mates, stud muffin. Total soul mates."

His lips pressed together tightly, and he didn't reply. She'd wager emotion overwhelmed him. Her evil overlord was so sensitive like that.

Soon, he'd have a way to express it in a bodily fashion. But before they got to the good stuff, they napped. And waited.

And chatted.

Waited some more.

Napped again.

Then she got annoyed. "When are we getting fed?" She paced her cell. "I'm getting very, very hungry."

"You sounded like that Martian fellow on *Looney Tunes* just now."

Her glare should have lasered him like an alien weapon. "Mocking my hunger is a bad idea, *muffin*." She might have drooled as she growled the word.

"You won't have to wait much longer, psycho."

"Don't you try and butter me up unless it's real butter. In that case, toss some over." She usually preferred a bit of popcorn with it, but she would make an exception in this case.

"Shhh."

He'd shushed her.

Without his cock.

Didn't he know how it was supposed to be done?

The slow, plodding step of Jabba zipped her lips. Given their earlier plotting, she cocked a hip, wet her lips, and was ready when he appeared.

"Hey, good looking." She eyed his empty hands and screeched, "Where's my fucking food?"

Okay, so the plan for seduction was off to a rocky start. The secret—one she didn't tell Samael about—involving blood and violence, though, was looking better and better.

When all else fails, dine al fresco. Jabba tartare is sounding good right about now.

She approached the bars and licked her lips. "Sorry about that, Jabba. I get a little testy when I'm hungry."

A little? The male voice laughed in her head.

"The suzerain wants you." Jabba eyed her, as was fitting.

She tossed her hair. "Suzie can kiss my perky ass. Wait." She frowned. "He already wants to do that. On second thought, tell Suzie to blow himself because these lips belong to Sammy."

"You think you have a choice?" Jabba snickered. "Night-night princess." He poured powder into his hand from the satchel at his…not exactly a waist. Roll by his side? Starboard section?

The fine particles flew through the air, a hazy mess of dust that she knew better than to inhale. She waved a hand frantically. Held her breath. Pinched her nose, and puffed her cheeks.

The fine dust landed on her skin.

Her eyes shut, and she sagged to the floor as the locks tumbled and clicked, the door inching open.

Only when Jabba was right over her, grunting—rudely—as he pulled her feather-light body—lighter than he implied, goddammit—did she snap open her eyes and yell, "Boo!" before swinging her legs upward and kicking Jabba in the head.

Rolling to her feet, she punched Jabba again and again. Giggling all the while.

"Drug me. Ha. My mother made me immune to most potions at a young age." Not always intentionally. Deka liked to swallow the stuff in the pretty bottles, especially if it glowed.

"Don't. You'll. Fuck." Jabba couldn't finish a sentence, and soon couldn't stand. He slumped to the floor, unconscious.

She put a foot on him and raised her hands in victory. "And the crowd goes wild."

When no applause was forthcoming, she glared at Sammy. "Ahem. I said the crowd goes wild."

He crossed his arms. She knew that look.

The kind that said he wanted to thank her in person rather than waste his energy clapping.

"I'm coming for you, Sammy." And she meant that quite literally. Shudder.

Chapter Ten

Nothing like the emasculating moment when you realize the petite and curvy woman, incarcerated less than a day, had a better plan for escape than you.

As they wandered the halls of the castle—free because of her actions—she asked, "Are you sulking?"

"I'm not sulking," he pouted, the gravity working overtime on his lower lip. "I still don't understand how Jabba's shit didn't knock you out."

"Practice, stud. I'm sure over time you'd have built up the same immunity to drugs that I have. Keep in mind, my mother is an alchemist. I've been inoculated and rendered immune to a host of things."

"Did you have to go take care of the other jailor on your own before releasing me?" Despite his repeated yells, she'd sprinted off—with the fucking keys—to knock out and drag back the other jailor. They were both now locked in her cell.

Then, and only fucking then, had she released him.

The shame of it.

"Don't pout, stud. I was just doing my honorable duty to my Sept by keeping the king's brother safe."

"Bullshit. You want me to owe you."

"Well, duh. You know as well as I that it's all

about the win. Now, are you going to wax on some more about my most eloquent escape or join me in completing it?" She held out her hand. "Let's blow this joint."

Almost, he reached for her hand, only to recall the mind-wiping experience of it last time.

If she touches me, I might not remember what I'm supposed to do.

And that's a bad thing because?

He couldn't afford to be muddled right now. Freedom awaited.

Brushing past her, his body shivering in awareness as skin rubbed against skin, he stalked the hallway of his own volition.

Go back. If the suzerain catches you roaming, you'll be in so much trouble.

Shut the fuck up.

"Who is that talking?" she asked.

"Stop listening to my thoughts."

"Stop shouting them then. Not my fault you're noisy. Which, I will add, I don't usually mind when it's about me and only me. But in this case, you are replying to someone else, and I don't like it."

"What are you yapping about now? I'm not talking to anyone but your crazy ass."

"And the voice inside your head. Who is it? I warned you about my jealous side. Mind-speaking should be something for you and me alone. No one else."

He paused and whirled. "What are you talking about?"

"That voice. You know the one that wants you to be a pussy. Who is it?"

"Me." The shame of it burned, acid tearing at his insides.

She shook her head. "No, it's not. Don't tell me you thought it was?" She snickered. "Silly dragon. How could you not realize someone screwed with your mind?"

You mean it's not me telling myself to wuss out and show my fucking belly?

Don't listen to her. She knows not of what she speaks.

Who the fuck is in my head?

Dumb question. Only one person would screw with his thoughts.

"That fucker." No wonder Samael kept rolling over. He wasn't truly listening to himself. Someone pulled his mental strings. "How do I get rid of it?"

"What do you mean how?" Her lips pursed. "Did no one teach you to guard your mind?" She made a disparaging noise. "Of course, Parker and that uptight bitch priestess didn't."

"Tell me how to make my thoughts my own. Lobotomy? Maybe if you punched me in the face. Just try not to break my nose. It is rather perfect."

Her lips twitched. "Almost as perfect as mine. As for owning your mind, it's rather simple, actually. Tell yourself the world revolves around me."

A frown creased his brow. "The world revolves around me? That's it?"

"No, silly muffin. Around *me*." She jabbed at her chest. "Although, you will meet some dragons who will try and convince you that they are the center of the universe. Totally false. It's me. Always has been."

She certainly was a shining light in his current existence. Still, it seemed too simple. "How is focusing on you supposed to help?" Then again, when he narrowed his view on her, everything else faded into the background: danger, his depression, wisps in the wind; however, focusing on her did make his throbbing cock and balls situation more pronounced.

"It works because, once you accept that I am the center of your universe, then you'll know the only voice you should listen to is mine. Anyone else, you can ignore."

Listen only to her? But she thought he was worthy of fighting for. She wanted to do decadent things to his body.

And he wanted to return that favor.

But still, making her the sum of his existence? Wasn't that trading one prison for another?

"How about I stop listening to all the voices in my head and instead do what I want." Because, hold on a second, as a Gold dragon, shouldn't the world, nay the entire universe, work around him?

"Are you disobeying me?" Deka whirled, green eyes flashing, lips curved in a smile.

How sexy she appeared.

And dangerous.

"It's not disobeying if I refuse to acknowledge you're more important than me. Actually, I will note that you are the one being rather impertinent with a Golden heir." The arrogance felt good slipping from his lips.

"Does this mean you're going to punish me?"

Bend her over my knees and slap her ass.

"Yes!" she growled, reading his thoughts.

She threw herself at him, slamming him into a wall, pressing herself against his body.

"What are you doing?" he asked.

"It occurred to me that while we're practically engaged, we've never kissed."

"We're not engaged. I never asked you to be

my mate."

"Semantics. We're meant to be together. If it makes you feel better, how about we take a modern approach. Hey, Samael D'Ore, wanna hook up?"

In a sane world, he would have said no. Then again, sanity was totally overrated. He palmed her ass and lifted her and murmured against her mouth, "I want to fuck you until you come so hard you can't scream."

A distinct shiver went through her body, vibrated into his hands, and trembled against his frame.

So sexy, which was why he kissed her.

He did.

First.

Finally, something he could claim as a win over this woman.

Except, while he might have started it, the mere touch of their lips rendered him incoherent. Pleasure suffused every ounce of his body. His nerve endings tingled. Golden power rushed through his veins.

He throbbed with need.

Yet she pushed away.

"Come back here," he growled.

She danced out of reach as he grabbed. "Not now, stud muffin. We have an escape to master. But hold on to that thought for later." She winked.

Fucking winked instead of taking care of the turgid problem jutting from his body.

He peeked down at his poor cock.

Soon, buddy. You heard what she said.

He was pretty sure someone sobbed.

Given he had reasserted some measure of dominance—*I am, after all, brother to a king*—he followed the pert ass ahead of him. It was only right that someone led the way and heralded his approach.

Despite having only been taken through the gauntlet of halls twice—once there, once back—she seemed to unerringly know where to turn. In short order, they'd left the cool temperatures of the basement levels below the castle for the more ornate and slightly warmer corridors of the main level.

Where they would usually turn left at the alcove with the basin of flickering blue flame, she turned right.

"Why are you going this way?" he asked.

"Because the other way went deeper into this castle and upstairs. We want a door going outside."

"What's wrong with a window?" He gestured.

Deka slowed and eyed the dusky gray curtain that spanned ceiling to floor. The thick material fell in heavy pleats.

"The windows probably have bars."

The lame excuse caused him to frown. "Why do I get the sensation you're reluctant to see the outdoors?"

"Because I have a feeling I know why my crew hasn't come to save me. And you won't like it." She yanked on the curtain and drew it open.

The vista outside beckoned, and he looked upon the barren gray wasteland with its red-rimmed rifts and stormy sky to realize, even as she said it, "We're not on Earth anymore, stud."

Chapter Eleven

"What do you mean the tracker isn't working?" Aunt Xylia barked at her laptop. The usually calm and staid elder Silvergrace was completely losing her shit.

The video conference call with Aunts Valda and Varna showed them frazzled, their platinum hair sticking out on all sides, their cardigans stained with meals. They'd obviously been working on the problem but didn't have the answer Xylia, or anyone for that matter, wanted.

Varna replied. "I mean, according to the satellite signals that were logged, her last recorded position is the one we gave you."

Turning around in a circle, pointing her laptop camera at the cow field they stood in, Xylia snapped, "As you can see, she's not here."

"Perhaps the chip was removed?" Babette offered.

The Aunts V managed to stare at her, disdain in their gazes clear, despite the laptop screen. "One does not simply remove one of our chips."

Valda sniffed. "Not to mention, they're specially designed to immediately notify us the moment they leave living tissue."

"What about an EMP?" Babette asked, putting her Star Trek knowledge to good use. "Would it wipe the circuitry?"

"Not likely. These were specially designed to ensure that the humans couldn't simply disable them and start nabbing us without us being aware."

"Well, something happened to fuck up your signal," Xylia snapped while Babette gasped—in delight. It was rare that an aunt lost her cool and swore.

It didn't last. Xylia sighed. "Excuse my language." She pulled a flask from her pocket and chugged it with a grimace. Apparently, the punishment wasn't just for the younger dragonesses.

"What about magic?" Babette asked.

"It could be magic, I guess." Valda frowned. "But it's rather rare for this time. I think I've only met two human mages in my life. I've never heard of a magic that can stifle technology. Blow it up, yes. But change its properties…" She shook her head.

"What do we do now?" Xylia paced in the field, agitation over her daughter's disappearance clear. "What if that disgruntled Golden dragon brother of Remiel's has her?"

"Then she'll be happier than a pig rolling in warm mud and be pissed if we save her." Babette's contribution was met with a glare. "Just saying, Deka is convinced he's her mate. If they are together, then be prepared for a fight because if she's claimed him, she won't give him up."

"If she's claimed him, then there will be problems. We already have a Golden male in the family. Not to mention a purebred king."

"But he's over in the USA."

"Your point being?"

The focus of all the eyes made Babette nervous, and yet, she owed it to Deka to try. "I'm saying that, back in the day, even the Goldens had to split their power. The high king ruled over all the Septs, but he had ambassadors in the different countries to rule in his stead."

"Are you advocating that Samael, after everything he's done, should be forgiven and placed in a position of power?"

"Um, yeah?" She didn't quite manage assertiveness with her reply.

Yet, Auntie still beamed. "What an excellent idea and solution."

Aunt Vanna snickered. "And this has nothing to do at all with the fact that your daughter would end up more powerful than our sister Zahra."

"The thought never crossed my mind." Xylia's false claim went well with her rapacious smile.

The dragons might unite under one color, but at heart, the hunger for power—and more treasure—ruled them.

"I hate to ruin this love fest..." Anyone could tell that Yolanda, Babette's own mother—the lovely pastels in her hair not entirely faded—didn't feel sorry at all. "But what if the child isn't fornicating with the half-breed Golden? She could be in trouble."

"You know she's in trouble. Especially if she is a prisoner of the red-eyed creature who killed the priestess." Deka was always in trouble. She just usually had Babette by her side sharing it.

"If that *thing* is involved and still using wyverns to do her dirty work, then that would explain the lack of scent." Aunt Xylia crouched to the ground and sniffed, her eyes flaring green as she drew on her other self. "It is as if Deka traversed this field, barely leaving a trace, then disappeared into thin air."

"You think they flew off with her?" Babette frowned. "But how does that explain the lack of signal?"

"It doesn't. As of right now, we have no proof as to who is involved."

"Deka's gut—"

"Is not what led her to France. A dead end is what brought her." Xylia fixed Babette with a stare. "I know about the crate and its disappearance. I also know my daughter was gallivanting around the city, declaring to all who would listen that she was looking for Samael and not keeping her own origins quiet." The stern rebuke had Babette eyeing her toes.

They could really use a new coat of polish.

Perhaps she should have tried harder to… Damn, but Auntie was good. She'd almost managed to make her feel guilty.

Straightening, she held her head high. "Deka was acting because no one else would. What if that red-eyed doppelganger did steal Samael?"

"Let us take your theory one step further. What if that doppelganger now also has a Silver daughter? Can you imagine the havoc she could cause with Deka and Samael?"

For a moment, there was silence as they imagined it. The glorious chaos that would ensue.

Funny, but Babette wasn't all that worried about her best friend and cousin. Deka, on her own, could get into tons of trouble with very little help— also known as tons of fun. Add in a Deka in love, and some red-eyed she-bitch getting in the way?

Shit could get scary, real fast.

"We'd better crack out the leather." It could handle blood better than any polyester rayon blend.

Eve Langlais

Chapter Twelve

Sitting on the throne, Deka watched Samael pacing. He did it so well, the muscles of his body taut, his expression grim, the loincloth he'd fashioned around his hips not fooling anyone.

I know what you're hiding down there, stud. A treasure for the sucking.

And suck it she would if he ever stopped agitating long enough to notice they were alone.

You should have ravaged me by now. She thought hard at him, and he didn't miss a beat.

The man was good. Oh so good. But he couldn't resist her forever.

"How the fuck are we supposed to escape?" he muttered for the zillionth time, instead of what he should have been saying, namely, *bend over, cutie pie, and let me take you to heaven.*

The man really needed to reassess his priorities.

"Calm down, stud. We'll figure something out."

He fixed her with a fiery green gaze, hinting of red. Was this place contagious?

"I am perfectly calm considering I've been taken prisoner in an alien dimension."

"I don't know if I'd call it alien." No tentacles or bug-eyed people so far. "It kind of resembles the biblical version of Hell."

"Not helping."

"Neither are you, I might add. We've been out of our cells a whole thirty minutes, and you've yet to try and seduce me."

He planted his hands on his hips and huffed. "Is that all you can think about? Sex?"

She blinked and smiled. She also might have stretched inappropriately. "Yeah. And judging by the boner between your legs, so are you."

His hands dropped over his tenting cloth. "Would you stop distracting me? I need to think."

"Maybe," she said, bouncing off the throne and approaching him, "you'd think better balls-deep in me."

"Exactly how is that supposed to help?" he grumbled.

"Because then you might get some blood back to that brain of yours."

"Did it ever occur to you that, at any moment, someone is going to notice we've escaped our cells and come looking?"

"Totally." She grinned. "The thought of discovery is rather titillating, don't you think?"

"Does anything disturb you?"

"Nope. And I'm surprised you're so bothered. The old Samael wouldn't have worried about getting caught."

"The old Samael was in a position of power. I could do whatever the fuck I wanted, and none would gainsay me. How do you think I got away with killing Parker?"

Her eyes rounded. "That was you!" she gushed. "Epic. So you can turn invisible? Why the heck haven't you tried to sneak up on me and goose me then?"

"Because it's not that easy to do."

"But you can do it?" she prodded. "And other stuff? You're a Golden dragon. Most powerful of our kind."

"Half Golden."

"That didn't used to matter to you."

His expression twisted. "I know, and because of my old arrogance, I screwed over the only family I had. Did things to Sue-Ellen I shouldn't have and basically alienated everyone who might have been on my side."

"I'm still on your side."

He stared at her, his expression blank, his eyes shuttered. "Why?"

"What do you mean, why? That's a very loaded word, you know."

He scrubbed a hand through his hair. "Why are you so interested in me? I'm not a king-in-waiting anymore. I'm not even a full-breed Gold."

"Gold enough for me."

"Is that all I am? A stud for you to fuck?"

"Well, you are a stud, but I will add that I no longer have to mate with a dragon by the age of twenty-eight. I don't have to mate at all. Yet, I intend to. With you."

"Why? What do you have to gain? I am a fugitive from my own kind. A prisoner of a creature that is probably demonic in nature. I have nothing to offer."

"That's where you're wrong, stud muffin. I think you've plenty to give a girl. And I'm not just talking about your body or your golden-caped swimmers."

"My what?"

"Can't you just focus on the fact that I want you?"

"No." Again he rubbed at his hair and tugged the ends. "I can't focus on it because I can't understand it. I have no kingdom in this place. No riches."

"Excuse me, but you are plenty rich."

"How do you figure that?"

"You have me." The biggest treasure of all.

"How does having you help us escape?"

"Because one and one is two."

"You can count. Give the princess a ribbon."

"Use your head, muffin. Before, you were fighting alone. A single planet with no sun to revolve around. No purpose."

"Is this another emasculating way of explaining what a better fighter you are than me?"

"I think you'll be a great fighter once you learn to let go and truly embrace who you are."

"And who am I?"

She stepped close and stared him in the eyes. "You are Samael D'Ore, one of the last true Golden sons and heir to the Golden throne should something happen to your brother and his fragile little baby."

"You're not planning to kill it, are you?"

Her tight smile revealed nothing. "You are a powerful man in your own right. A dragon beyond compare. You have powers some of us can only imagine. Inner strengths you've yet to tap. And a smokin' body I want to lick."

Oops, she might have said that last part aloud.

Given how he kept fighting her allure, the last thing she expected was for him to grab her and draw her close. His strong hands clasped her firmly around the waist and lifted her on tiptoe.

His gaze bored into her. The swirling depths a chaotic green and red storm that churned. Parts of her churned, as well.

Especially her girly parts.

"How is it you drive me so wild?" he finally asked, his stare not wavering. His focus on her proved intense, and she thrived under it.

About time he finally *saw* her and reacted as he should.

"The reason you're feeling weird and mushy stuff, my stud, is because you recognize me as your mate. The reason for your existence. It must be overwhelming, after all. My level of awesomeness will only come to you once in your life. But I want you to know that I'm okay with you worshipping me." Magnanimous of her. *I know. I'm just so giving that way.*

The corner of his lip lifted. "You are stunningly arrogant."

"Thank you." She might have tilted her head in a preening motion. Her lips parted seductively, and she made sure to glance at his mouth.

Any second, he was going to lose control and kiss her.

Any second.

His lips moved…in order to talk!

"The logical side of me says I should ignore your considerable charms and try to find a way to escape."

"Boring," she sang. Who wanted logical when he called her charms considerable?

"Yes, boring, because who wants to play it safe?" His brow arched most pointedly. He was fascinating to watch.

"I always vote for danger." She threw that out there because, hello, apparently, some short-lived exbeaus thought she was a little too quick to say yes.

To anything.

Those who refused to participate, she dumped—but only after she got them to hold her beer.

"I knew you were going to say danger. In some ways, you're predictable."

"I resent that."

Again, his lips quirked. Parts of her quirked, too.

Will he ever shut up and kiss me?

Had she said that out loud because, all of a sudden, his lips went insanely wide, his eyes shone with red fire, and he held her tighter in his arms.

The proximity set off shivers in her body.

"Kiss you or escape? The choice should seem obvious," he whispered, the words hot against her lips.

"I think we can all figure out which one I'd choose," she murmured back, brushing her lower lip against his with the last syllable.

His turn to have a fine tremor run through him. "It boils down to giving in to desire or being smart."

"I think it boils down to kiss me or I will hurt you badly." Deka's patience only went so far.

"I already ache. Which is the entire problem. I also can't think around you." He nipped her lower lip.

She might have melted in her panties a bit.

"Just kiss me already."

"I'll kiss you when I damn well please," he growled, brushing his mouth across her cheek to the corner of her mouth then stopping.

Fingers clutched his shoulders, dug into the taut muscle as she hissed. "Who do you think is in charge here?"

A whispered *you* floated across her mind, yet his mouth moved to say, "As you keep pointing out, I am the Golden dragon here."

"You are."

"Which means, I bow to no one."

"About time you realized it." She beamed at him.

"It also means, as the highest-ranking dragon, you should be obeying me."

"Let's not get hasty there," she said, rubbing her mouth against his lower lip, hearing him catch his breath.

"Obey me, *woman*." The way he said it made her insides flip.

"Ha. Not likely. I'd rather plan an escape first. Then again... I don't know why we're even thinking of escape when—"

"—we can take over." His lips stretched. "Now why didn't I think of that?"

"Because you're a man, and I am a goddess."

"Did you just elevate yourself to outrank me?"

"Just pointing out the obvious. Agree or not, at your peril." She bit his lower lip, tugging it and pinching tightly.

His hands slipped from her waist to cup her ass, squeezing the globes. "You are ridiculously bossy, and it should be so unattractive, but fuck me, I can't resist you." He kissed her, and she let out an inaudible happy sigh.

Some women might call Samael crude and arrogant in his mannerisms. They just didn't understand a real man. He was strong enough to be her equal. He wouldn't just give in. Nor would he chicken out if things got difficult.

As he continued to kiss her, his hard mouth slanting over hers, Deka melted. Good thing she'd ditched her panties or she'd be wringing them out.

He lifted her up, and it was instinctive to wrap her legs around his shanks, to draw him close to her.

Stupid loincloth was in the way. She could only feel him through the fabric, rubbing against her wet slit.

Reaching down, she snared the impediment and ripped it away.

He grunted.

It was a very sexy sound. A primal sound.

She trapped his turgid cock against her, the moistness of her sex sliding along him, a tease for them both. Her skirt rode around her waist, allowing her to truly angle her legs and body the way she wanted, finding the tip of his cock, right at the juncture. The pulsing heat of him pressed.

She wanted him inside her so badly. She started tightening her legs and drawing him in. A gasp escaped her, and a moaned, "Yes. Yes. That's it."

"No one warned me I'd be getting a floor show," said Suzie, who was now wearing tits again. The bitch's arrival totally threw off the flow of the moment.

Deka rotated her head, and yes it was probably very exorcist style. She couldn't help her aggression, given her body pulsed in need and this ho was interrupting.

Like, hello, couldn't this next scene of overdone evil have happened after she got laid? It would have taken like what, two minutes tops?

Fucking pain in my ass. I am going to kill her, or him. I'll kill them twice.

Deka's legs unwound from Samael's waist as

she dropped to the floor. She stood in front of him, not so much protectively than as a measure of modesty.

Suzie'd better not be looking at my mate.

Kill those that covet. Crazy Great Aunt Helga taught her that. She also taught her to smuggle her own snacks to the theater rather than pay those outrageous fees.

"I have to say, I am impressed that the girl thought up a way to get out. She didn't seem that bright." Suzie's cloak snapped around her frame as she stalked closer.

"So, when you call me bright, that's a good thing, right?" Deka took a few steps and smiled the smile Aunt Helga had also taught her.

It made big dogs whimper.

For a second, Suzie wavered, the lines of her body blurring, showing something more, bigger, darker with horns, followed by a fuzzy Hermie, then some dark-skinned chick before snapping back to Suzie.

"Stupid, Silver dragon. I will make you pay."

"So stupid I got out of your prison super quickly. I would have been out earlier, but I needed a nap."

Suzie's lips flattened. "You couldn't get out earlier. Why do you twist things?"

"What did I twist? I took a nap. When I woke up, I escaped." It seemed obvious to Deka. Samael might have coughed behind her. Probably getting a cold from the draft going to his cheeks.

I should be warming those cheeks.

"Return to your cells or face the consequences." Suzie stretched her arm, the cloak dripping shadows underneath it.

Deka clapped her hands. "Oh, goodie, a game with a prize at the end. Let me guess the rules. For you to win, you need to put us in our cells." Her gaze turned serious. "As for Samael and me… To win, we just have to kill you." Smile. "Bonus points if you scream."

Because here was the thing. While good guys were about justice, Deka wasn't good, and she had no problem making her enemies cry—or, even better, bleed.

Chapter Thirteen

What the fuck is happening? Samael listened to Deka—a petite and curvy woman with sex appeal so great he still had a hard-on despite the interruption—threaten to rip out the intestines of the suzerain and wrap her in a bow.

Talk about bat-fucking-shit crazy.

And violent.

And so fucking cute it hurt.

She was unlike anyone he'd ever met, and he couldn't help but want to toss her over a shoulder to take her somewhere he'd never shared with anyone.

But he would with her.

If they made it out alive.

Perhaps the suzerain was having an off day, or perhaps Samael had finally opened his eyes. Whatever the reason, Suzie didn't look as powerful as he recalled. The cloak, however, did have some major cool mojo.

Want it.

Take it.

The voice was Deka's, and her advice agreed with his desires. He took a step forward, only to have Suzie narrow her gaze and snap, "Don't move." She gripped a pouch with a drawstring by her side.

I recognize that bag. The same one the Jabbas used. Inside, glittering sand that, when inhaled, turned him into a pathetic prisoner.

You can't escape. It's impossible. You know what will happen if you do.

He remembered. Remembered the agony as he sagged in chains.

You don't want to do this. You know the pain you'll suffer. Is it worth this small moment of rebellion?

Rebellion would hurt, and hurt for a long time.

Better to behave. Give yourself up. Convince the girl to give herself up, too.

The very idea of handing her over had him cocking his head, and he couldn't help but mentally blast, *Like fuck am I giving Deka to anyone.*

His silver-haired princess angled her head and replied as if she heard him. "Of course, you're not giving me away. You're gonna keep me exclusively as yours forever and ever. Aren't you, muffin?" She batted her lashes at him. "And if you don't kill what's keeping us apart"—Deka cracked her knuckles, the perfect manicure at the tips of her fingers a nice touch—"then I will."

Suzie's red gaze turned to her. "You will come quietly, Silver, or I will have him take you and show you just how unimportant you truly are. My pet knows who his master is."

The Silver is a troublemaker. You should help get her back to her cell before she causes you more pain.

The Silver?

He would never call Deka, that fiery-hot woman, something so generic and tame.

But Suzie would.

And in that moment of recognition, the suzerain lost her power.

He glared. "Get out of my head."

"You need to listen to me, or I will hurt you."
She raised a hand.

A very small and pale hand.

It could inflict a lot of agony if it chose.

So could he.

He lunged and tried to grab the suzerain;
however, the smoky cloak passed like mist through
his hand.

"How dare you." The magic hit him and threw
him across the throne room as if a giant fist of air had
grabbed him. He hit the pillar hard enough to hear it
crack.

"Don't you touch my muffin." Deka flowed
forward, and while the suzerain formed balls of light
that she flung, Deka dodged and ducked, a primal
sound—was it laughter?—coming from her lips.

As he stood, he couldn't help but watch as
Deka's forward rush forced Suzie to trip backwards.

"Freeze." The word flowed out of the
suzerain and hit Deka, who shivered and slowed for
only a half-second.

"Fuck you, bitch." Deka began to glow. She
wasn't hampered by the side effects of any drugs.

She could change at will, and the suzerain
realized it too late. Something blasted from her hand,
but that didn't halt Deka's transformation, her figure
expanding, her scraps of clothes shredding.

He could feel the metamorphous charging the
air, the lightening of pressure as her body expanded,
the shape of her filling out, becoming buoyant. The
inside as if a hollowed drum. The distributed weight
was part of how their wings worked with their size.

But in that lightness there was strength. A
transformed Deka, her silver scales edged in hints of
blue, chased after the suzerain, who dodged behind

pillars, lobbing magic.

Whereas he, he gripped the collar around his neck, the fabric coating on it enough to keep him from burning but not enough to prevent the magic from impeding his own ability to become.

I can become in my cell. The collar didn't stop him then.

When angry. But right now, he wasn't the one who was pissed. That was Deka. She trumpeted as she chased the suzerain out of the throne room via a small door behind the throne. The move momentarily foiled Deka, whose wider dragon body got caught in the slim arch.

A smart man, he knew mentioning it would only result in his certain death.

He risked it anyhow. "Gonna have to wiggle that ass of yours a little bit more if you want to fit."

He was pretty sure she gave him a mental finger.

"Need a shove?"

Yeah, that whack on his mind was definitely a tap from her.

He grinned.

"Maybe you should try another door. A wider one."

He clearly heard her mutter *like hell* that time.

Watch and learn, muffin.

One moment, she was solidly jammed; and the next, she became liquid silver. The shape of her turning slightly amorphous then flowing like a river of mercury through the doorway.

Fucking cool. He'd never seen the likes of it. It meant, though, that she popped out of sight.

He jogged to catch up, entering the hallway to see Deka sliding around a corner.

He ran and almost made it before the crackling sound started.

Why does that seem so familiar?

Didn't he recall the smell of cow manure and fresh soil on a night with thunder and lightning?

Hitting the bend, he slowed, only enough to pivot, then keep bolting, seeing massive portals ahead that opened onto the nightmarish landscape.

A way out.

Mauve lightning, with hints of blue, crackled down from the sky. Jagged forces of electricity that hit the ground and bounced. One after another, they struck.

Going out would mean avoiding them. He would have rolled up his sleeves if he had any because he was about to play the ultimate game. A game of dodge the electrocution.

Rushing to the door, Samael didn't notice the body until it hurled itself into his side.

The momentum took him into the wall, and air whooshed out of him.

For a second, he sucked hard to get it back. He shoved the heavier body off him, revolted by the stink, utterly repelled by this thing. One of the Jabbas, surely a native of this place.

But it didn't explain the eyes.

Why do I feel like I know those eyes?

"Get off me, lardo. Or I will wring your fat neck."

He could have, he wasn't powerless, not anymore, and yet he didn't. And before anyone called him sentimental—*I should spare my jailor because he never technically hurt me but took care of me in his rough and gruff way*—yeah, that thought never entered his mind.

He kept Jabba alive because it was practical.

He might need someone with answers about this place. Flipping his jailor onto his back, he pinned him, hand pushing against a throat. The clammy skin had a rough quality to it. It squished as he pushed, and Jabba stopped struggling.

"Do it. Kill me." An odd request.

Instead, he relieved some of the pressure. "Why do you persist in working for her?"

"Because we have no choice."

"There is always a choice." He would know. He usually went with the wrong one.

"For a long time, she was the only choice. And now, she is too powerful to gainsay."

"Unless you side with someone to take her down."

"Someone like you." Jabba chuckled, a rusty, rotten sound. "I'm not stupid enough to ally myself with you. With all the essence the suzerain has imbibed, she'll be too strong to beat."

"What are you talking about?"

"Her power. It keeps growing the more she feeds. It heals her. Makes her strong. Immortal."

"No one is immortal."

"Because the cost of drinking another's soul is too high for most people."

"She's a vampire?"

"She is much more than that. She is dragonkind's worst nightmare."

"The same could be said of you." He pressed down, and Jabba's face turned a shade of purple. The stubby arms flailed, and the body under his began to go limp before he eased up. "How do we get out of here?"

"Through the stone portals in the courtyard. But you're too late."

"Too late for what?"

"To save your friend. Why do you think she had me waylay you?"

The truth hit him hard. Jabba was a distraction. The suzerain had split them up on purpose in order to go after Deka.

A trumpeting clarion drew his attention. Deka's battle call.

"Deka will be fine." The violence in her matched his. Yet, would it be enough to win? "She's strong enough to handle it. I managed to survive."

"If you think the suzerain will be content to sip from her, then you are mistaken. She sipped from you in order to preserve you and keep feeding on you. A feeding to the death is the way to madness. But, in your friend's case, I don't think the suzerain will care. She's already gone mad."

The very thought of someone killing Deka by taking her soul didn't bear contemplation. No. He wouldn't allow it to happen. But he had to know one thing before he ran off to save her and then bask in her thanks.

"What is the suzerain? And what are you for that matter?" he asked.

Why the familiarity?

Of course, when Jabba finally told him, it made so much sense. But Deka didn't know. He had to tell her.

He punched out the Jabba and leaped to his feet. He ran outside, only to skid to a stop on the stone dais. The lightning crackled faintly in the distance.

There was no carnage to see. No dead bodies, but rather a very alive Deka standing in front of a shrinking portal, waving.

Alone.

Also very naked, which meant his dick began waving.

He dropped his hands as he approached and asked, "What happened to the suzerain?"

"Suzie escaped," Deka exclaimed as she whirled and planted her hands on her hips. "About time you showed up. You missed all my great moves."

"Not so great given you let her get away."

"Let her?" Her chin angled. "I fought hard, and valiantly."

"Says you. When I showed up, you were waving."

"You mean gesturing rudely because I'd just finished telling her what I would do when I caught up with her." Deka blinked her lashes—*that's right, muffin, I told her what was what*—and he frowned.

"How did she escape? What is that thing?"

He strode toward the stone circle, held upright on a huge dais of rock, the surface smoothed, and yet the lines in it carved deep, inlaid with a burgundy color. Counting, he noted thirteen hoops spread around. The stone felt warm under his touch.

"I don't know what it is exactly," Deka explained, "But it worked like some kind of portal."

"Out of here?" he asked sharply.

"That's what it looked like. Alas, it closed. Which means, we're stuck here. All alone. Just the two of us. Whatever shall we do?"

Finish what we started. Duh.

He couldn't have said if the thought was his or hers. Did it matter?

Chapter Fourteen

"Why in tarnation was Deka grinning like a fool?" Yolanda asked, the slightest of creases marring her brow.

"As if you don't know," Babette snorted. "Surely, you're not that dense, Mother?" Just in case, she might have done a hip sway and sung a few bars of Bow-chica-wow-wow.

The exaggerated sigh was totally worth it.

"Who was the naked man behind her?" Aunt Xylia asked.

"Who do you think it was?" Then again, the scruffy beard made it hard to tell. The fact that they'd seen anything at all was a surprise. With the empty farm field a bust, they'd regrouped at the hotel. It was Aunt Xylia who returned at the insistence of Aunt Valda to set up surveillance in case there was an entrance to a hidden underground base. Those existed a lot more than people realized.

The tripod and camera they'd left behind hadn't caught a single thing but buzzing bees and butterflies until the interdimensional rip opened!

That caused quite a stir.

"We should have set up base camp in the field," Xylia grumbled, miffed they'd not stayed behind. However, in their defense, they'd not exactly expected a portal between worlds.

When the dark doorway opened unexpectedly, with a crackle of lightning in a cloudless sky, it set off the alarms on their video surveillance system. Shoving each other out of the way, jostling for position, they'd crowded around the laptop, only to gape in astonishment as the very air itself turned into an opaque portal that gave a glimpse into another world.

A hellish-looking world with a stormy sky split with jagged branches of lightning, ancient-looking monolith-type rings of stone, and the hint of a castle beyond it.

So freaking cool.

A figure, the eyes a bright red, the cloak billowing in true super-villain fashion, swept through the rip.

"It's that bitch who delivered us Anastasia's head!" Babette remarked.

As if any of them would ever forget those glowing red orbs.

The woman in the cloak, which danced around her like ephemeral strands of smoke, paused only a moment to look behind through the portal at the world she fled. A doorway that showed—

"There's Deka!" Babette pointed to the silver dragon that flowed into view.

"Shhh."

They kept watching, and through the shitty video feed saw Deka pause instead of coming through. Shifting to her human form, she glanced over her shoulder as if looking for someone. Then, instead of stepping through the door, she waved and mouthed something.

The portal shut. But Babette would have wagered Deka was fine with that because she'd found her Golden prince. Actually, Deka's exact mouthed words were—as Aunt V later deciphered through the use of video replay and lip reading—"Having the time of my life. Tell Mom not to worry."

But that was later. In the here and now, they sat around staring at the screen, showing once again a cow field with scraggly grass and flitting butterflies.

Of the red-eyed woman, nothing. Of Deka, also no trace. As for the doorway, examination by the finest equipment couldn't detect it.

Later that day, hands on her hips, Babette's mother surveyed the field. "I hate to break it to you, Xy, but I don't think we're gonna be able to crack it open."

Aunt Xylia grimaced. "Bloody magic. Give me a good ol' potion with actual ingredients any day over metaphysical crap."

"Auntie!" Babette gasped. Just because it was fun to watch her take out the flask and swig from it.

"Good thing you told your daughter to stay away from that Gold."

"So predictable, eh?" Xylia retorted. "Nothing like forbidding a child to make them do the opposite."

Yolanda snorted. "You're telling me."

The meaning of the words jolted. Babette eyed her aunt. "You did that on purpose? You wanted her to find Samael?"

"Of course, *we* did." Her mother smiled slyly. "Just because Zahra doesn't want Samael found on account of her daughter being married to a half-breed Gold, and because she's allied herself with the king, doesn't mean we don't want the same prestige for our daughters."

"Um, I don't want to marry a guy." That had been an awkward conversation a few years ago.

Babette thought her mother understood her preference.

"Not you, silly. Deka. My girl could be queen." Aunt Xylia rubbed her hands, and the glee practically dripped from them.

"I can see why Auntie would want to do this, but why are you helping?" she asked her mother.

"You're Deka's best friend." Mother shrugged. "Have I taught you nothing about grabbing power? When you spot a chance, always ensure your hierarchy in the Sept." Because much as it was about family, even within the family, there was an echelon, and remaining in the top spots took maneuvering.

"I'd say given the lack of clothes on her, and his definite displacement of them"—giving them all an eyeful of his assets, enough to make Babette happy she went another route—"that things are going well."

"Think he'll manage to impregnate her before they figure a way out?" Yolanda asked, tapping her chin with a finger.

"Knowing Deka, she's already screwing him and making sure he doesn't even think of opening that door," Babette declared. "But I have to say, aren't you guys worried at all about the fact that the crazy red-eyed chick is back?"

"Bah. What can one female do?"

Words they would come to swallow as that one chick, and her blazing orbs, sent out her army of humans armed with guns, her wyverns armed with teeth and claw—and Molotov cocktails—to start an Armageddon.

The Septs hadn't been this excited in years. Decades. Centuries. And the old leather armor and light metal plates were dug out and polished for battle.

Chapter Fifteen

Meanwhile, back in the hellish dimension…

Despite his massive hard-on, and their previous interrupted make-out session, Samael didn't immediately pounce on her.

Playing hard to get. It only made her hornier. He insisted on securing the castle—including locking up the Jabbas that Suzie had released—checking all the rooms for more soldiers—none were found, but the remnants of clothing in dusty drawers indicated that, at one time, the castle had more occupants.

He insisted on going through the place, room by room, top to bottom, then through it again, although the second time, she let him go alone. Especially since she'd found the kitchen.

When he finally rejoined her, it was to find her in a food coma on the throne, her hands over her round belly, a sappy smile on her face.

Suzie had left the larder well stocked.

"There's no one else in this place," he declared, stalking in wearing an unfortunate amount of clothing, AKA pants. He'd left his upper body bare, which only served to enhance the sheath he'd found to hold the giant sword lying down his back.

"If it isn't my studly Conan back from protecting the realm." She waggled her brows. She blamed the wine she'd found.

"Aren't you curious at all as to what I discovered?"

"Expressing keen interest is for those who don't know everything. As the center of the world, I know it all."

"Did you know there's an abandoned village just past the castle?"

"I do now." She smiled and scooted over on the throne. "Why don't you come sit here and tell me more?"

"We should be looking for a way to escape."

"You're right. We should. And we will after you take a rest. You must be tired after all that protecting."

He eyed her, and his damned pants hid what he thought, but his eyes glowed green with a hint of red. "How come you didn't get dressed?"

"I had more important things to take care of?"

"Like?"

For one, washing her hair, shaving her legs with a sharp knife because, hello, not in Paris anymore, getting some food in her tummy and… She leaned over behind the throne and pulled out the temptation.

A plate with a stacked sandwich. She waved it in front of him, and he took a step forward then another until he could snatch it from her. When he plopped down on the steps of the dais to eat it, she flowed out of the throne and kneeled behind him, feeling the light tremor that went through him when her fingers began to knead the muscles of his shoulders.

"Playing servant?" he said between bites.

"Hardly. I try to exercise my hands daily to

keep them limber. Since my usual equipment isn't available, your body will do."

"Do?" He chuckled as he reached behind and drew her onto his lap. "Don't think I'm not aware of your tactics."

"You'd have to be pretty blind not to see what I'm doing." She cupped his bearded cheeks. "So, are you going to keep playing hard to get, or do me?"

"You call that being sexy?"

"If you wanted sexy, then you shouldn't have teased me for so long."

"We barely know each other."

"Discovery is part of the fun. And do you always have to know your partners before you screw them?"

"But you've said it yourself, you want more than sex."

"I want you."

"What if we're not compatible?"

She slapped him.

It didn't actually hurt, but his jaw dropped. "What the fuck?"

"Stop with all this Negative Nelly shit. Evil overlords don't doubt themselves or their allure. Ever."

"They also don't let bossy women order them around."

"They would if I was the one giving the orders." She smiled and stroked the cheek she'd slapped. "Now, repeat after me. Deka is right."

"Deka needs to stop talking."

"You're supposed to be the badass here." She cocked her head. "Make me."

She expected more argument. She could see how verbal sparring riled and roused him. But even he'd finally reached the end of his patience.

His lips smashed down onto hers, a forceful embrace that stole whatever breath she might have had to speak.

Since she was already in his lap, it was easy for him to control the kiss. To demand more.

Instead, he rolled on the raised platform for the throne, his arm anchored around her middle as he shoved her to her knees.

Her hands reached out to grab the rim of the throne. She peeked over her shoulder.

"Is this where you punish me?" she asked huskily.

He crowded her, pressing in from behind, the rigid length of his cock trapped between her ass and his body.

He still had her anchored with one hand, and the other rose to slide through her hair and grab it, his strength, his grip making her a prisoner to his desire.

The fact that he thought he could control excited.

The reality that he might just be powerful enough almost made her come.

Excitement had her grinding against him, the cheeks of her butt rubbing his erection.

He uttered a low growl.

So sexy. He drew her ass farther out, and her arms stretched as he positioned her. She wore nothing to impede the fingers that slid from her stomach to her hip then stroked over her rounded cheeks. It took only the slightest tickle of his fingers to part her thighs.

Exposing her.

And as was only right, he stared. The heat of his gaze had her panting.

"Tell me why you came," he queried, his voice low.

"I came for you. Because we belong together."

"Have you ever done that for a male before?"

"Of course, not." She went to turn her head only to have the grip on her hair remain tight. She sucked in a breath. "I came for you and only you."

"I don't think I can give you what you need."

"I need you."

His turn to inhale sharply. "You make me want..."

The thought was never finished as he traced her damp slit with the tip of his finger, a light touch that brought a delicious quiver.

"I want this. Touch me." With him, she would beg.

He listened and turned bolder. His fingers penetrated her sex, plunging into her heat, and she couldn't help but moan at his touch.

In and out he pumped as her breathing hitched and she rocked back against him. He thrust his fingers deep, his hand cupping her mound as he shoved into her, roughly. The way she liked it. He made a small noise of pleasure as he did it, in time to his thrusts, and her head bowed as she felt bliss building inside.

Then he stopped.

She might have growled.

Then she cried out in pleasure as he replaced his fingers with his tongue.

"Yes. Yes." She couldn't help but chant as he deftly traced her sex. His tongue slipped into her, teasing and probing. He flicked her clit until she gyrated, shoving her ass out, needing that rhythm.

Over and over, he sucked at her clit, teased it

into swollen delight. Sexual tension built inside her.

"Fuck me," she begged. "Give me that beautiful cock."

"Come on my tongue." The command tore what shred of control she had. She came, screaming loudly, her body clenching in orgasm as he continued to tongue her, drawing out her pleasure, stringing it so tautly she gasped and cried. "Enough. I can't. No more."

He paused his licking to murmur, "Yes more." He blew on her, and she shuddered at the promise in his words.

He moved, and the tip of him pressed.

"Yes!"

The head of him slid and teased across her swollen, wet sex. He grabbed hold of her hips and sheathed himself, deep and filling, oh so filling.

The wideness of his cock stretched the walls of her channel. Gave her something plentiful to grip. Her pussy suctioned him tightly as he thrust, in and out, his pace starting slowly but quickening.

He slapped in and out of her, his fingers digging deep into her flesh, his breathing ragged, as labored as her own, and her throbbing body quickened.

The steady rhythm stoked her desire until her body tightened for a second time. She screamed, loudly, as her second climax hit. Her whole body seized, and he uttered a sound as his own orgasm hit.

Heat bathed her womb.

Deep satisfaction curved her lips.

She practically collapsed from pure sexual bliss. Her head hung low, and her breath was ragged, but that didn't stop her from screeching when his hand slapped her ass and he commanded, "Fetch me a sandwich, princess. And this time, easy on the mayo."

Chapter Sixteen

After that first time in the throne room, he ate many sandwiches, in between fucking Deka senseless.

He enjoyed the latter more than the former, which was saying a lot because she actually made a pretty mean sandwich.

In between the sex and food, he explored. The mystery deepened the more he searched.

The castle proved ancient. As in stone crumbling with age, some rooms covered in a thick patina of dust, ancient hieroglyphics.

Taking his time to go through dressers and wardrobes meant coming across strange garments, some disintegrating at his touch. Most had a medieval feel to them, the skirts long for the women while, for the males, the breeches were snug and usually laced. Only in Suzie's quarters did he find signs of modern wear, for both male and female. But no cell phone. No way to contact the outside world.

No answers to anything.

There was a library in the castle, the tomes, covered in some strange leather, almost like dragon skin yet not, inscribed with strange runes. Since he'd studied archeology what seemed like a lifetime ago, he had plenty of experience with archaic languages, yet he couldn't decipher a thing.

Nor had he yet discovered what lived, or used

to live, in this world. Because Suzie wasn't the only sentient creature here. The abandoned village showed signs of once having been inhabited, but not by humans.

The chairs had no backs; everything was a stool. The doorways were tall—taller than he was used to seeing. And there were no beds, rather strange bars suspended overhead, almost like perches for bats.

But no bats. Nothing lived in this barren world. Nothing except him, Deka, and the Jabbas.

The first few days, he didn't pay his former jailors much mind. He treated them as they'd once treated him. He tossed them bowls of gruel and occasionally set off the sprinklers—their hollers at the cold cleansing douse bringing a grim smile of satisfaction to his lips.

The days fell into a routine where he woke and fucked Deka senseless. Then she'd make him breakfast—from supplies that dwindled—then off he'd go exploring, claiming he was searching for a way out.

He found it, and rather quickly, too.

Turned out the portals weren't all that hard to activate. But…he kept that a secret for now because he was having too much fun.

For the first time ever in his life, Samael could do what he wanted. He worked, fucked, or did nothing at his leisure.

There was no one around to give him orders except Deka, and those were usually of the erotic variety.

No one to punish him for wanting to be his own man.

No one to be jealous of.

No one around to make demands of him but Deka.

His Silver princess.

She, on the other hand, kept trying to find a way out, claiming they needed to escape. Although he would add that she didn't try very hard and was easily distracted.

Look, a romance novel I've never read—the Jabbas' bedrooms proved full of them—and off she popped to read for a few hours. He didn't mind because, once she got to the dirty parts, she always came for him, eyes alight with need and hunger.

Dirty, hot, sweaty, and erotic hunger.

Fuck it felt good.

No wonder he didn't care if they ever escaped. But the food dwindled. And he was running out of places to explore. He even took to playing checkers—the board created on the stone floor, the pieces the cracked bones of the cooked bird he'd brought the brothers—with the Jabbas when Deka thought he was valiantly searching for an exit.

In case anyone wondered, he wasn't softening on the Jabbas' incarceration. He still didn't trust them. But he had no problem buttering them up to get information.

Jabba One—whose real name turned out to be a rather banal, Maedoc—happened to ask about two weeks into their Hell vacation if Samael had been keeping up on the news in between banging his girlfriend.

Yeah, my girlfriend. He'd agreed to that much at least in the face of her persistence.

Pausing the game, Samael glared at the male, who didn't appear as putrid with regular bathing and a clean robe. "What do you mean news from the outside world? I thought we were cut off." He moved a fragment of thick bone to a spot and watched the rib with a little bit of gristle adjacent from it.

"Did you not wonder at how Suzie"—the Jabbas had adopted the name—"was so well informed?"

"Not really." Because he'd been self-involved with screaming most of the time.

"I know you've been exploring. Did you not wonder at the number of mirrors in the small parlor?"

"Um, no." Because he'd assumed they were for kinky sex. It was how he used them. Taking Deka on the one settee in there meant he got to see her from any angle he liked.

His Silver princess was so beautiful when she came.

"The largest, most ornate mirrors are tuned to different worlds, and some of the smaller ones surrounding them to different places in the same world."

"Why?" He watched Maedoc move a chunk of leg across the board.

Excellent. Samael made his next epic move.

"Knowledge is power. Even though she was imprisoned here, the suzerain always kept well informed for the day she could escape."

"Why wait? Those portals outside aren't that hard to activate." A few of them at any rate. Some remained dark, no matter what he did. He just wished the lightning wouldn't crackle when he played with them. He kept expecting Deka to notice, yet whenever he experimented, he returned to find her napping soundly. And then, because she looked so temptingly soft, he usually fucked her.

"Those portals work in phases. The one she

originally came through went out of alignment shortly after. It took her centuries of waiting before the cosmos moved close enough again for her to create a portal back to Earth."

"Centuries?" Samael frowned. "Impossible. You told me she was a dragon once upon a time." The revelation still shocked him. "We age better than humans, but we're not eternal."

"Have you not guessed her secret to life yet?" Maedoc mocked him. "For a scientist who specialized in the past, you're not very astute."

"I still don't know if I believe she's a dragon. Her eyes are all wrong."

"You mean the red irises?" Maedoc shrugged as he moved another piece. "The solitude of this place and her diet changed her."

"And made her live longer?"

"The dark magic she's discovered is what extended her life."

Samael questioned, and for once, Maedoc answered. What he didn't understand was, why? "How come you're revealing this to me? How do I even know you're telling the truth?"

"You don't. However, it occurs to me that my brother and I will probably die in this place, and I find myself unwilling to let our story die here, too."

"You aren't going to die." He'd even thought of letting them go once he and Deka left.

"Our fate is sealed. As is yours if you don't leave before the portal between this world and Earth shifts. The other planets you can access can't sustain our kind of life. And we've stripped everything we could from this one. Once the planes move out of alignment, we will have no access to food and starve."

Samael absently moved a piece on the game

board as he absorbed the information. "In other words, it's time to move on. What if I took you with me?" Again not altruistic on his part at all. The Jabbas had knowledge to impart, and knowledge was power.

"We cannot leave this place. It is part of our banishment."

"Who banished you?"

Maedoc looked him in the eye with a gaze so familiar that he wasn't surprised when he said, "The Septs did. The suzerain wasn't the only dragon abandoned here."

He eyed the tubby male up and down and then snickered. "Dragon, my ass. If you're a dragon, shift."

"I can't. Not anymore."

"Because you're lying. First off, dragons don't live centuries. Two, they don't have red eyes, and three, I'm pretty sure if a bunch of dragons had been exiled for crimes, we'd know about it." Almost being wiped out didn't mean their legacy had died. From a young age, they were taught the history of their kind. Hammered with the mistakes of their ancestors so they wouldn't make the same errors again when they rose to power.

"Our existence was wiped from the annals. No one wanted to remember the truth."

"And what is the truth?"

"The suzerain, who started her life as an Orange dragon of the Ochre Sept, was a sorceress."

Huge snort. "Dragons aren't witches." They had unique and special powers depending on their genetic color blend, but it was their nature, not mystical power.

"Are you going to listen or just disparage every word I say?" Maedoc's rebuke emerged tersely.

"You're asking me to listen to a fairy tale."

"No, I am asking you to listen to a truth that has been hidden and buried for a long time. Once upon a time, certain dragons, a rare number of us, wielded magic. But we were banished after the purge by the humans. All dragons exhibiting the slightest hint of magical ability, down to the smallest child, were exiled to this land."

Samael wanted to deny it, and yet there was a somber quality to Maedoc's claim. A truthfulness he couldn't deny. "Why banish you?" he asked.

"Because our own people feared us." He snorted and shook his head. "Feared us because of a single sorceress who singlehandedly destroyed our people."

"The humans destroyed us."

"Those puny creatures?" Maedoc snorted. "The humans had help. A dragoness sorceress was the one who brought back the metal the humans used to kill us. From this very realm, as a matter of fact. Then she further abetted her crime by aiding the humans, giving the location of the lairs to them."

"Why the fuck would she do that?" A betrayal of that magnitude shocked even Samael. He'd only locked up his brother, never machinated his death. Nor the deaths of hundreds.

"Jealousy. The fact that a suitor spurned her advances. She wanted the Golden king to marry her, but he chose her sister. And so she sought revenge. She didn't live long to gloat about it. Her own sister was the one to track her down and rend her limb from limb. It wasn't enough to save us. The actions of one doomed all the sorcerers of that time."

It took only a short moment for him to reason out the why. "The Septs had to eliminate all the magic users because they knew how to get more of the metal. That kind of power..." The temptation of knowing a plane where you could get the one weapon that would make you a ruler over all the Septs...

"Now you understand. All of them had to go. Even the queen and her little magic-using daughter, who had nothing to do with the crime. In order to prevent any more fighting and truly decimating the few dragons that were left, the queen led the way through the portal to this plane, along with as many supplies as they could manage."

"If they knew how to open it, couldn't they have just returned?" He had a hard time fathoming people who would sacrifice themselves.

"The queen's honor meant everything to her, she had a way of speaking that made you believe in her. By the time we realized the hell chosen for us, the planes had shifted. The way home was blocked."

"And you all should have died of old age, but didn't. How?" This was the crux of the story.

"While we had food to sustain our bodies, mortality stalked our kind. As we grew older, there was a desperation to stay alive. To extend our life any way we could. The queen forbade it. But once she died..." Maedoc shrugged. "We didn't all have her fortitude. We chose survival."

"But how? You're talking about living centuries past a normal life span. How is that possible?"

A snort shook the male. "Magic, of course. Magic that we found here in our prison. Once we discovered it, we didn't hesitate. At first, we stole life from others. Using the portals to invade the other planes when they rolled into position. We hunted down the living, bringing them back that we might feed."

"You ate them?"

Maedoc snorted. "Don't be dense. You've seen how it's done. Seen how the suzerain uses her magic to imbibe your essence. It's dark magic, the darkest kind, and yet, it was all we had. That and a will to live. Some of us were so young when shoved into this prison for the simple crime of being born. We didn't want to die for the sins of others." The resentment still burned in Maedoc's words.

"The world has forgotten what happened. No one knows. Why not start over? If you don't like this world, then why stay? You said you have access to other places—"

"Uncivilized planes, none of which promised the possibility of one day going home. Dead worlds now. Stripped bare of all life in order to extend ours. In our arrogance, we never thought to keep breeding pairs to sustain ourselves. Kind of shortsighted if you ask me. But at the time, we never expected our exile to last so long. And as our soul supply dwindled and age once again crept, we turned on each other."

"You cannibalized each other?"

"Not at first. We borrowed essence back and forth, only to have the lack of fresh souls fail miserably. We changed. Became unrecognizable." Maedoc looked at his body. "That was when the madness set in, and the killings began until only three were left."

"Three?" He eyed Maedoc and then behind them at the other cage with Eogan, his brother. "Three fucking dragons. I don't believe it." Couldn't believe it because looking at them was peering at a perversion of life itself.

"That is the problem with the young

nowadays, no respect for the word of their elders." The disdainful remark floated to them across the way, and Samael scowled.

"You have to admit your story is farfetched, starting with the fact that you don't look anything like the dragons I know. Or smell like them for that matter." Rather a putrid scent that no soap or water could rinse emanated from them, one like overripe flesh.

"Because once we began to feed back and forth, we were, in essence, starving. The perversion of essentially eating ourselves caused us to shift. We lost touch with our dragon and became grotesque."

"Suzie isn't nasty."

"Because she committed the ultimate travesty. A century ago, she began picking off those exiled with her. Treated us like a buffet, and with each complete soul, she changed. We might have lost the ability to change into our beasts"—a hint of sadness there— "but she gained the ability to shift into whatever, or whomever, she liked. A true doppelganger. But one who grew increasingly madder. The curse of killing while feeding."

"If she ate all your buds, how come you're still kicking around?"

"Because she needed servants. In the past, we had others to do chores, creatures brought from other worlds to serve her."

"They were delicious," Eogan added with a dark chuckle.

"I'm still not understanding something, though. You said the planes shifted, that she had access back to Earth. So why kidnap me? Or Deka for that matter?"

At first, he thought Maedoc wouldn't answer,

and that meant he'd have to grab him by the throat and toss him against a wall a few times to make him speak. But he wouldn't enjoy it. He kind of—very little mind you—liked the guy. Dragon. Thing. Whatever.

Eogan replied. "Suzie, as you call her, is preparing for the end of times. As this world drops out of alignment, so a darker realm takes its place. The horsemen will soon ride and, in their wake, will sow pure chaos. She wants to be part of that."

"So she's what, preparing for Armageddon? Is that why she's got those humans and wyverns doing her bidding? And how did she find them anyhow?" It wasn't exactly easy to build an army. Samael had learned that the hard way.

"She has the gift of compulsion, and those with weak minds fall sway to her will." Eogan approached the bars and gripped them. Samael found it interesting to note that, despite their so-called dragon heritage, they didn't cringe or react to the metal.

Then again, I don't always react either.

"Suzie is strong. Stronger than even she realizes at times, I think. As the youngest of those banished, she's been collecting souls for a long time. A few in battle. Most by subterfuge. But as she learned early on, taking from the weak resulted in weak results, and she's not interested in weakness. She wants to rule the world. You asked why come after you and the Silver girl. Because you are the strongest of the colors."

But she'd never had a chance to snack from Deka.

Just me. "All this time, she's been eating my soul." It explained his depression. "How do I get it back?"

"There is no getting it back, unless you want to use the same dark magic, and I personally don't recommend it. But good news. A soul, given time, will regenerate, but slower and slower if continually damaged."

He bounced a glance between the brothers. "Why are you telling me this? Why now?" He'd been visiting them daily with their meals for two weeks. Playing games for the past few days. Exchanging insults and barbs. This spewing of information appeared out of nowhere.

I didn't even get to torture them for it.

"Perhaps there is a semblance of honor in us that cringes at the fact that you allowed a mad dragon back into the world. We were banished so that magic would never cause the fall of dragonkind again, and yet, because we chose not to die, because we fought and killed and stole to stay alive, we've contributed to the very reason we were banished."

Eogan began to cackle, a hint of madness in the sound. "Voadicia, the one styling herself as the suzerain, is going to set the Earth on fire. And it's all your fault."

Take the blame? Hell, no. Samael shrugged. "How is it my fault? She was popping in and out of her prison before I came along."

"You should have stopped her," hissed Eogan. "It is the duty of the Gold to protect the dragon Septs."

"I'm a half-breed, remember? My brother is there to deal with it."

"A true Gold leads; he doesn't sit back."

"Can't exactly lead from here." He gestured to the cell.

"You know how to leave this world. You just choose not to because you're too busy dipping your wick," harrumphed Maedoc.

"You also know how to leave, yet instead you chose to serve that psycho bitch," Samael retorted.

"Leave and go where? Have you seen us?" Eogan remarked, pointing to his corpulent shape. "We are no longer the men or dragons we used to be. We are grotesque monsters. In this new world with humans on edge, and the masses set to revolt, how long do you think we'd last?"

"Isn't there a cure?"

"Were you not paying attention? How do you think Voadicia regained her true shape?"

"You said she ate the others."

"She did, and yet they were as grotesque as us. It wasn't until the portals aligned and she got her first taste of a fresh subject that she discovered the secret, thus beginning her cannibalistic feast."

It didn't take a genius to clue in. "Eating fresh dragons brought her back. She's been picking us off. How the fuck did no one know?"

"People go missing all the time. A few here. A few there. It's not as if they left a trace once she brought them here."

"You joined her in dining?"

"I'd like to lie and claim we were too honorable to eat our own kind, but the truth is"— Maedoc shrugged—"she wouldn't let us."

"Would you have done it if given a chance?" There was something kind of vampiristic about it.

"What do you think?" Maedoc glared with disdain. "At this point, the only way we can hope to return to our former glory is to imbibe the souls of dragons. Many dragons. Who would condone us sucking the souls of others to save ourselves?" The lips pulled into a blubbery smile.

Samael shrugged. "I can't deny the will to survive to anyone." Because dropped into the same situation, he'd have probably done anything to remain alive. And more.

Eogan cackled. "It's too late for us. They were right to damn us. And we should have taken our punishment and died as expected."

"But we didn't," grumbled Maedoc. "While it's too late for us, you can still effect change."

"What if I'd rather not?" Going back out there meant the same shit pile as before.

People who hate me.

People who want to kill me.

People who hate and want to kill me or cut me up for science.

Then there was the brother he probably should apologize to. Not that Samael had done anything wrong, but the big jerk was being a baby about the whole locking him up thing and hitting on his woman thing and he kind of expected it.

Then there was the fact that he'd told everyone he was going to be king, only now, he wasn't. He was—gack—a nobody right now.

Untrue, you're the brother to a king. A Golden in his own right.

The world is big enough for two.

If it didn't burn first.

He frowned, and Maedoc took the chance to bounce his chunk of rib bone around the board and elegantly beat him.

Again.

Asshole.

He got to his feet. "I need to check on

something."

"You won't find any annals to corroborate our story."

"I don't need one." Because the longer the Jabbas spoke, the more their story rang true. Samael didn't know if it was a Golden power, or just the fact that he could read their intent, but they weren't lying.

Which meant a great evil had been released upon the world, and they might not even know it.

The room of mirrors Maedoc mentioned proved easy to activate once Samael knew what he was looking for. It took but a rub of the sand-colored jewel crowning the top of the mirror to ignite the magic.

The sizeable glass illuminated, as did the reflective surfaces nearest it. Their faces filled with a desert of black sand that undulated, swirled in gusts of wind, and, at times, even turned into dark holes that closed without a trace.

Not earth.

He moved over and activated another gem, a crystal-clear one. Frozen tundra, snow of palest mauve piled in drifts, the branches of trees, heavy with icicles that jangled as a breeze shot through them. Round humps gave the impression of buildings, yet not one track marred the snow.

A water world next, just endless waves.

An orange jungle of trees, bereft of life.

Then the world he both sought and dreaded.

Earth.

The largest mirror showed an abandoned temple, parts of the ceiling caved in, a place long forgotten.

The mirrors scattered around the large one seemed to be dotted throughout the world.

The perspective for most was from on high, as if the image were anchored from the sky.

They showed cities with their towering skyscrapers, roads meandering with cars that crept like little ants.

In many, smoke rose in spirals.

Was this the anarchy Maedoc and his brother spoke of?

It's none of my business.

He kept repeating that to himself and was so focused on it, he missed her arrival until she said, "Guess we can't avoid going home anymore."

"You do realize home is about to turn into a war zone. We'll probably die."

"Or, we could save the world."

"Fuck 'em. Leave them to their fate." They never cared about his.

"And miss out on the killing?" Cocking her head meant Deka's pigtails bobbed most enticingly. He knew what he wanted to be for Halloween this year and what she should wear to match him. Maybe he'd recreate the scene where he shoved the girl off the platform then dove after her.

He eyed her.

Deka smiled back and mouthed, "I'll grow out my hair for longer pigtails by then."

The damned woman was reading his mind, again, wanting to fulfill his fantasies.

"There might not be a world by October."

"Ye of little faith. I'm pretty sure you and I can handle Suzie."

"Suzie's been gobbling up souls for breakfast, lunch, and dinner to get stronger."

"Yeah, but here's the problem, muffin. She messed with us." Deka smiled. "And I think we're owed some payback."

The thought of revenge did sound sweet.

"How do you know all this?" he asked.

"You're not the only one who knows how to question prisoners."

He glared at her. "You knew and didn't tell me."

"You're the one who keeps telling me you're so great."

"As I recall, you're the one who started calling me god in bed." And against the wall. And on the throne.

"A god shouldn't need his woman to tell him anything." She ran a finger down his chest. "Or are you admitting I'm better than you?"

"I know what you're doing," he growled as her hands reach around to cup his ass.

"I know that you know that I know what I'm doing."

"You're using sex to distract me."

"No, I'm using sex because I'm horny."

"Much as it pains me to admit, we need to go back."

"I know. I know everything," she said with a laugh, sliding her hands inside the waist of his pants to cup his butt.

"If we do go, then what do we do about Maedoc and Eogan?" Because, while he'd like to trust them, they had, after all, eaten dragons and anything else they could get their hands on to stay alive.

"Who?"

He didn't want to say it, but... "The Jabba brothers."

She snickered. "Are they still kicking around? I guess we can let those leeches go. But only after we save the world and I show those heifers my Gold is better than theirs. Shall we open the portal?"

He blinked at her. "You know how to open those, too?"

A smirk pulled her lips. "You aren't the only one who can decipher ancient instructions, stud. Wait until you hear my repertoire of dirty languages in bed."

Speaking of bed, soon he'd have a real mattress under him, not that weird stuffed shit that passed for a mattress here. Because they were going home.

To save it.

Which meant work and not a lot of free time.

Before they left the mirror room, he fucked Deka twice.

And when he found his release inside her from behind, he almost bit her. Almost put a mark on her that would have bound her more surely than anything else.

But he held back.

How disappointing.

He couldn't have said whom the thought came from. He didn't care.

She's mine.

All mine.

Yes, yours.

Dun-dun-dun.

Chapter Seventeen

What a bummer. Not only had Samael yet to mark her, but their emergence into the real world proved free of fanfare.

Deka planted her hands on her hips and glared at the empty field. "Where is my welcoming committee?"

"Don't you mean, where's mine? The prodigal Golden prince returns. That merits at least an emissary." Samael did look rather regal in his ancient garb of tight blue velvet britches, ivory shirt edged with tattered lace, and supple black boots.

She, on the other hand, wore a modified princess gown, the skirt shortened and the cleavage hacked. "Those lowdown heifers. They're jealous, stud. Jealous I tell you."

His chin took on an arrogant tilt that she wanted to nibble. "Of course, they are, because you get to be with me. You're welcome."

"Excuse me? I chose to be with you," she said, managing an even more imperial cant of her head. "You should thank me for coming to find you. After all, it was my brilliant plan that brought me to that dungeon to save your sweet ass."

"I could have saved myself," he grumbled.

"Sure, you could have." Smirk. "So which way do we go now, muffin?" She turned to look at him over her shoulder and thus missed the box camouflaged in the high grass, which tripped her.

Lightning-fast reflexes meant he caught her before she landed on her face.

"Aha, I just saved you. You're welcome. Now we're even."

She cast him a glare through the hair in her face. "I wouldn't call this even."

"You're right. I'm probably slightly ahead. You can thank me with head later."

"You'll be lucky if I don't bite you."

The leer and his husky, "What if I want you to bite me?" almost sent her swooning face first again.

Releasing her slowly—to her utter disappointment because, hello, they could have been fucking in the farm field—he dropped to his haunches to study the weather-tight box.

"What do you think's inside?" he asked.

"The heifer's idea of an emergency pack," she muttered. But where was her family? Last time she'd peeked into the field there was a tripod set up with a camera. Now…nothing but a strip of charred grass east of them, the smell of old smoke tickling her nose, and the more putrid stench of rotting flesh.

A battle had happened here. Who'd won?

She stood rather than open the box and peeked around. There was something eerily quiet about this spot.

The flat field had nowhere to hide. No rocks to mask an ambush. No trees for people to spring from behind. The grass, for the most part, appeared undisturbed and untrampled, and there was nothing to indicate anything belowground.

Yet…she could see the wasteland, a dark scar amidst the lush green. A burnt swath.

Of the camera she'd waved at before, not a sign. Nothing but the box.

"There's no one around for miles," he stated.

"How can you tell?"

"Because I can feel it."

"But say that person was shielding themselves? Like in a lead box? Or a blind?"

"We're alone."

"But—"

"How about you don't question? I know because it's a weird skill Anastasia had me cultivate."

"Along with the invisibility thing."

"Among other things."

"You'll have to show me those *other* things." And yes, there was innuendo in those words.

She dropped back down to the grass and slapped his hands when he would have undone the hasp on the box.

"Don't. It could be rigged." Rarely did a dragon leave treasure out in plain sight without at least something to scare off the unworthy.

She ran her hands over the box lightly, feeling for any vibrations—she still remembered the bee incident in the cookie jar. Damned Aunt Yolanda's way of catching the cookie thief.

She waited to see if her hands would tingle from electricity—battery-operated traps always had a hint. She leaned closer to smell, although not all drugs could be scented that way.

"Oh, for fuck's sake. It's a goddamned box." He tore at the latch and threw open the lid. A smart dragoness—with a pretty face—she threw herself behind him.

"Did you really just use me as a shield?"

"If the width fits…"

"What happened to me being a Golden heir? Shouldn't you be jumping in front of me?"

"That only applies to women not sleeping with you."

"Since when do we sleep?"

"Good point."

Together, they peered into the disappointing box. In a *Ziploc* bag on top, a note in elegant script.

About time you're done with your little vacation. The Septs are at war. Mostly with the being calling herself Voadicia. No last name, which is utterly pretentious. Probably a peasant. We have been by the field sporadically to clear out welcoming committees. You're welcome. I'll expect you to check in the moment you arrive. There's a phone at the bottom. Your loving mother, X.

"I just got the warm and fuzzies," he exclaimed.

She cast him a side-eye.

"Not." He smirked. "Better call your mommy."

"Don't be a dick."

"Kind of hard not to considering its size."

Again, good point. Under the bag, she found two more, one with a cell phone, the other with a set of car keys.

"Nice of them to leave us some wheels," he remarked.

"They could have left me some lipgloss, too." All that kissing was leaving her chapped.

As they began to walk toward the road and the shadow parked on the shoulder of it, she couldn't help but stare at the sky. A cloudless, blue sky.

She distrusted it. It just seemed too easy.

Way too easy.

Samael didn't peek once. He just walked all ladi-da, not a care in the world.

"Why isn't Suzie here?" she asked. Surely, the crazy cow had to know Deka would arrive to vanquish her.

"Probably because she's off enjoying her Armageddon."

"She should have left something behind, though. It can't be this easy. I'm kind of insulted." She peeked over her shoulder to see the grass unmoving, no sign of the portal. Which begged the question, how did it open from this side?

"There's a special word."

Having gotten used to him reading her thoughts, she wasn't too surprised. "What word?"

"That's for me to know, and you to fuck me into cross-eyed bliss to find out."

"You're on."

Halfway across the field, she could better see the vehicle left behind for them parked on the side of the road. A Range Rover. Nice wheels. Probably bulletproof.

But the real question? Was it flame retardant? Because that nagging suspicion turned into an aha moment as the charred ground burst open, the ashy dirt releasing several full-grown dragons and a few wyvern hybrids.

"Told you it was too easy."

Ditching his fancy jacket, Samael grinned, his eyes wild with green fire and a red glow. "Still is. See if you can keep up, princess. Or are you going to hide behind me again?" With that, he burst out of his clothes, the fabric shredding from his frame, his body expanding, stretching, and becoming immense, the smooth skin she knew every inch of turning scaly. The golden scales were duller than Remiel's with hints of another color, one she couldn't describe.

Of more interest, the budding horns on his forehead. The ones that seemed to grow a little more each time he shifted.

He was an impressive beast. Massive in size. His fangs the longest she'd ever seen. And he was fearless.

The cowering man she'd first come across in the dungeon, a man beaten physically and battered even more mentally, had recovered his mojo. Charging at their enemies with a trumpeting dare— hinting at darkness.

"Show them no mercy, muffin!" she yelled.

Aren't you going to help? was his query.

"You got this, stud. I have faith in you." And just in case he needed incentive... "I'm pretty sure that big red dragon is Jeremy. He tried to kiss me once."

The truth, in this case, didn't matter, just the result as Samael let out a huge blart of sound. He threw himself into the air, his body somehow twisting to avoid the stream of liquid fire aimed his way.

Most Reds tended to be rather bland with their powers. Fire for the most part. Boring!

But put several of them together, and things could get hot.

Samael didn't cower in the face of their attack, and seating herself on his jacket, which he had so kindly left behind as a blanket, Deka watched.

"Oooh, nice move."

Thanks.

Called out encouragement, too. "Rip open his underbelly." Messy but effective.

Anything else, princess?

"You're doing fine on your own."

Gee, thanks. No mistaking the dry retort.

She smiled. Who knew having a real dragon boyfriend would be so fun?

Who says I'm your boyfriend?

You did, remember?

He ducked under a stream of fire and rose up to club the other dragon in the face and then grab hold of the enemy's wing to tear it.

The ground didn't shudder despite the massive beast that hit it. Big didn't always mean heavy.

Boyfriend sounds so juvenile, he finally said, casting her a quick glance.

"I'm sorry, is the correct term fiancé?" He'd yet to ask her, but who needed to say words when it was unspoken?

You assume a lot, princess. What if I'm already promised? He grappled midair with a pair of wyverns who'd darted in to grab at his arms. A dragon rose from below.

It probably wasn't the time to distract him.

"Promised to whom?" she snorted. "We've been exclusive for more than two weeks. You've been missing for months."

Well, there were those other girls.

Her gaze narrowed—and not because the combined attack of the wyverns and remaining dragon managed to drag him to the ground. "What girls?"

But he didn't reply. He pretended to be fighting for his life, tearing, rending with his claws. Ducking blows. Grunting at others.

He shimmered for a moment and then disappeared from sight.

"You can't hide forever," she shouted. "You

will tell me." So she could hunt those women down and make sure they understood he belonged to her.

Kind of busy. Busy dancing among those that dared to stand against them, an invisible shape that slashed and killed until only bodies remained, wyverns and dragons who resumed their human guise upon death. Until there was only a Red left. Samael appeared suddenly, his golden claws tipped in black, gripping it around the throat.

The clarion of his question, *Where is your mistress?* Replied with a hiss.

He squeezed, and the other dragon thrashed, trying to grab the claws that held him, but Samael had longer arms than a normal dragon, stranger wings, too. And his horns…she'd have to tell him at one point about those.

The Crimson traitor died, its mouth opening on one last exhalation. One last jet stream of fire, which, of course, ignited the fucking Range Rover.

"Seriously?" Deka exclaimed, jumping to her feet. She'd been looking forward to air-conditioned comfort and seeing who'd hit the top one hundred while she was gone.

Moments later, silence reigned until a big-assed Golden dragon landed in front of her.

She jabbed him in the plated armor of his chest. "So, about those women…"

He shifted back, compacting all that lovely airy strength into one tight and sexy body.

"What about them? You weren't the first chick in that cage. Suzie brought in plenty. Not all of them dragons either. The suzerain enjoyed fresh meat. Apparently, she'd seduce them earthside then bring them through the portal. They never lasted long."

"Did you fuck them?" Deka might have kind

of grabbed him around the throat and squeezed. Might as well try to get water from a rock. He kept talking, despite the fact that she dangled from his neck.

"I'm not a whore. I do have some standards. Sniveling females tend to not make the cut."

"I don't snivel."

"No, you don't. You are rather magnificent in action."

"Thank you."

"But I'm better when it comes to action," he boasted.

"Are not."

"I'd argue, but it's pointless when you obviously know the truth. Why else would you resort to the meek flinging of words?"

"I'll show you meek," she growled, and she meant to show him how tough she really was, but then he swung her into his arms, princess style.

Yeah, she kind of melted at that.

"Nothing wrong with being delicate. You now have a big man to protect you."

She mentally hoarded it because it pleased her greatly. However, she had to reply. "What a ridiculously sexist thing to say."

"I know."

"I guess we're going to have to walk since someone"—she didn't attempt to hide the accusing glare—"didn't protect our ride."

"Maybe if someone had gotten off her lazy princess butt instead of cowering…"

"I was not cowering. I was applauding your valiant skills."

"Still looked like cowering."

"Says the man who let me chase after Suzie

alone."

"Men know better than to get involved in a girl fight."

"What if she'd turned into a boy?"

His eyes lit with triumph. "Are you saying boys are better than girls?"

"Oh, that was twisty, muffin. Well done. But you still haven't answered the question of how we're going to get to the closest Silver Sept safe house."

"We'll fly."

"In broad daylight?" she screeched.

"The world knows we exist now."

"That doesn't mean you should put yourself out in the open for everyone to see. And I might note the whole purpose of a safe house is to ensure you can hide without anyone knowing. Hardly hiding if we both fly to it and land with the whole world watching."

"First off, you're not flying. I'll be carrying you. It's the only way to make you invisible."

"Invisible?" Her eyes widened. "Oooh." She clapped her hands. "Can we take a picture?" She pulled out the phone she'd used to Snapchat the fight.

"You do realize invisible means no one will see us?"

Her cheeks might have heated. "Shut up."

He chuckled, the deep, masculine sound transitioning to a shivery fluting as he shifted to his dragon form. He held her cradled against his impressive chest and used his back legs to spring them into the air, and in a few pushes of his wings, they were airborne. And invisible, which was kind of cool, given she could feel her hands groping her boobs but couldn't see them.

"This is epic!" she declared.

Glad you like it.

"Do you know what would be cool? We should role-play. I'll be the innocent woman sleeping in a haunted house, and you'll be the naughty ghost who seduces me."

Does your mind ever stop?

"Nope." And she proceeded to regale him with other things an invisible man could do, from dropping condom-filled balloons on people in wide-open spaces, to sneaking food off people's plates, and of course, making love in the middle of a crowded room.

After a while, she did notice something. "Where are you going?" Because he wasn't following her directions to the safe house she'd mentioned. The long stint over the ocean made that very clear.

I know a place.

"If you know it, then chances are it's compromised because of the time Suzie spent impersonating Anastasia."

This place is a secret. You'll like it.

He wanted to show her a secret place? Another panty-wetting moment—if she wore panties. Which she didn't. Ha.

Of course, his idea of secret and hers differed apparently.

Their arrival proved less than exciting.

He landed after hours of flight, a portion of which she spent napping in his arms, in a field of golden wheat.

"You do realize if I were gluten allergic, you'd have killed me," she declared as she followed his naked butt through the waving fronds.

"I've seen the way you devour pasta."

"I'm a growing girl. I need my carbs.

He snorted. They left the field for a scraggy front yard, the grass losing the fight against the weeds. A sad-looking tree with half the branches bare and dead didn't encourage her to try the tire swing hanging out of it.

"Why are we stopping here?" she asked as she stood in front of the clapboard farmhouse, its paint—more gray now than white—peeling, the windows' wooden sashes split and, she'd wager, drafty.

"This is the place."

"This is your secret?" She could see why he didn't tell anyone. It underwhelmed.

"This, princess, is more than a secret." He turned around to face her, pride on his face. "This is *my* home."

She might have pulled something laughing.

Chapter Eighteen

"Don't sulk."

"I am not sulking," he announced, the words emerging petulant on account that his lower lip was strongly affected by gravity at the moment.

"I shouldn't have laughed so hard."

"You almost peed yourself."

"But I didn't."

He glared.

"Your home is, um…lovely, in a falling down, shack-in-the-middle-of-nowhere kind of way."

"Mock it all you want. It's mine."

"Mine's bigger. And newer."

"Bet it doesn't sit on three thousand acres of land." He'd managed to achieve privacy in a world where oftentimes there was too little.

She peeked around, hands planted on her hips, hips he'd held on to as he plunged his cock into her body.

Schwing. His dick didn't care if she mocked his farmhouse. It thought he should skip the bullshit and get to the fucking part.

She threw up her hands. "I'm sorry, muffin. I don't care if it sits on a jillion acres. It's flat farmland." She gestured with a hand. "There's not even a herd of bulls for me to play with."

"We can get horses." He gestured to the

dilapidated barn.

"I'm pretty sure it would be considered animal cruelty to put them in there."

"There're rabbits in the fields."

"This"—she gestured to her frame—"needs more than a rabbit. Give me red meat."

"I've got red meat for you." The hip thrust might have made another woman blush. She, on the other hand, licked her lips.

"I am a tad puckish." She took a step toward him.

He held up a hand to halt her. "Not out here. Someone could see us."

"Who?" Again, she gestured. "There's nothing for miles around."

"What if I said there was a bed inside?" He grabbed her by the hand and drew her to the house. She went reluctantly, and he grinned.

Such a spoiled princess. She saw only the worn-down aspects of this place. She didn't see all the other things that made it wonderful.

The door yielded at his touch. Why bother locking it? What could anyone steal?

Inside, worn linoleum greeted them, a faded brick pattern that never, ever, even when new, looked like actual tile. A glance to the left into the living room showed a room with ratty furniture, the stuffing oozing out of holes. The hardwood floors in that space had lost their veneer years ago and turned a dirty grayish tan.

The wallpaper, a running theme throughout the home, boasted a wildflower pattern faded with time, the edges of it peeled.

"Are you sure this place is safe?" she said, peering about with doubt.

"Structurally sound, I promise." He wrapped his arm around her waist and drew her close to him so they both stood in the middle of a braided rug that could have choked someone if they took the time to beat the dust out of it.

"What do you think?"

"I think you need an interior designer."

"Are you disparaging my hoard?"

"You consider this your hoard?" Her arched brows went well with her high-pitched reply. "You should think of taking lessons on what constitutes a hoard."

"Perhaps you can educate me in my bedroom."

"Is it on the second floor? Because I've got to say, I'd be worried all that bouncing around might send the house crashing down around us."

"Actually, my bedroom is below." He uttered a short note, a tiny whistle that caused the house around them to shiver then disappear as the carpet they stood on dropped down a hole, which immediately sealed behind with a new seamless section of floor and rug.

The entranceway to the true part of his home.

Deka squealed, not in fear, not his Silver princess.

She squealed, "I should have known you were screwing with me. This is amazing!" Her excitement proved contagious.

Down they plummeted, air rushing against their faces, her hair fluttering in a spiked 'do.

One story. Two. Three. His true home lay far underground, and no, he'd not dug it out himself. He'd found this cavern by accident when looking to buy a place that would offer privacy. He'd toured the less-than-impressive home, hemming over the choice, when he found the well in the cellar. He'd dropped a rock down it, only to never hear it hit. Being young and adventurous, he'd jumped down with only a flashlight.

He'd found something amazing.

The carpet halted on a stone dais, intricately carved and inlaid with gold. His true front hall, so to speak.

"Welcome to Maison D'Ore."

For a moment, she didn't say a word, just glanced around, taking it all in. "How did you get your hands on paradise?" The awe in her voice made him swell with pride.

"I was an archeologist. Remember?"

"For ancient places like Egypt and stuff. This is in the middle of potato country."

"The best things are sometimes hidden in plain sight." No need to admit he'd found it by a fluke. He didn't believe in coincidences. Fate, on the other hand, according to all his research, might be fickle, but she did have a purpose when she guided.

"How did you get a castle down here?" She stared at the edifice rising from the bottom of the cavern, the submerged lights in the pond to the left of it refracting on the stone.

"I'd like to take credit, but I found most of this as you see it."

"Who built it?"

He shrugged. "No idea. It might have been a dragon ancestor." And yet, the language he'd found, even some of the murals, indicated another race. Something no longer seen in this world.

"Are the lights magic or natural?"

"More like man-made. Anything modern or

electrical was a touch I added."

"All the perks of home," she murmured. "What about cable?"

"Of course. We have high-speed internet, too, courtesy of a satellite hook up. All the amenities you'd expect."

"But how? Did Parker help you with this?"

He snorted. "Parker was an abusive a-hole who thought he was in charge. I allowed him to think it because, as long as he thought I was a good little soldier, he tended to not pay much mind when I disappeared on digs. Sometimes for weeks without contact."

"And while you were faking him out, you were creating this." She whirled to take in more details before turning and slugging him in the gut.

He lost his breath and felt he should add she did not hit like a girl.

It was so fucking hot. He tossed her over his shoulder as he strode toward his domain.

"Aren't you going to ask me why I'm pissed?" she railed at his back.

"That would imply that I'm interested in hearing your reasoning, which is probably something inane, such as you're PMSing."

"I am not PMSing."

"Then I'll wager you're pissed because you were gullible enough to think I would actually live in that run-down dump upstairs."

"It's not nice to trick people."

"But it is fun," he said with a chuckle.

She snorted then laughed. A giggle cut short as he entered the castle and it illuminated, the subtle lighting he'd put in reacting to his presence.

"How does it run? Do you have a power plant

down here or something?"

"Or something," he said with a grin. "Those farm fields you see outside? Not all that wheat is real. Some of it is a fiber optic type of strand that absorbs solar energy and then runs it down to a rather large holding unit."

"I didn't think they'd created batteries big enough to hold much."

"Oh, they exist, but the power companies don't want you to stop relying on them. It's all about the money, princess."

"So your farm field is actually some giant electricity field?"

"It is. And this is my stronghold. My hoard. It can withstand any nuclear attack. Even an asteroid. If the world ends, we can watch and eat popcorn."

"With butter, I hope, because only savages eat it plain." The words didn't come from Deka, which was why he jumped.

How embarrassing to be startled. Then again, he never expected Babette to jump out of a doorway, can of soda in hand.

"What the fuck are you doing here?" he barked.

"Waiting for you." Babette shook her head. "Took you long enough. Did you take the scenic route over the ocean?"

"How did you know where *here* was? Tell me." He bristled as he advanced on Babette while Deka struggled on his shoulder.

"Don't you dare kill my favorite cousin," she squeaked.

"Maybe your favorite cousin shouldn't show up in a man's castle uninvited," he growled. But he set Deka down and contented himself with glaring over his woman.

"Calm down, stud muffin." Her small hands pressed against his chest. "I guess I should have warned you to expect her. Babette and I do almost everything together."

"Except guys." Babette shuddered. "I prefer something a little more feminine myself."

"How did you find my fortress?" Because if this dragoness had found it, then how long before others did?

"Through the hidden door."

"What hidden door?"

Babette rolled her eyes. "If I tell you, it won't be hidden anymore."

"How did you even know we were coming?"

"Would you like me to count the ways? One, the tracker in her ass reactivated." Babette ticked a finger. "Two. Cell phone signal." Deka waved the phone in question. "Which reminds me, text your mother. She's been a rampaging bitch these past few weeks. And three, who do you think sold you the solar technology, for a fortune that enriched our own coffers, I might add?" Babette uttered a loud ka-ching for emphasis.

He glared. "The Silver Sept is spying on me."

"Well, duh. It is our job to know everything that needs to be known to help out the king."

At Babette's words, he stiffened. "Does that mean Remiel knows I'm here?" Because he wasn't quite ready to deal with his brother. Give him a decade, or two, maybe even three.

"Not yet. But I wouldn't expect that to last long. The Aunts V are Zahra's puppets. Seeing how easily I found you, chances are they know, too, and they'll probably tattle before long."

"Does this mean Mother will be showing up, as well?" Deka asked.

Her mother? Oh, fuck, he wasn't ready to deal with a pissed parent. *Oh, hey there, I've been banging your daughter. Hope you don't mind.*

His entrails would probably make a mess on the floor.

Babette waved a hand. "Don't worry about your mom. She'll be a while still. I might have told her your tracker was spotted in Australia."

"Um, we are in Australia," he muttered.

"Yeah, but she thought I was lying, so she's combing Europe."

"Maybe she wouldn't have to go searching if she'd stuck around and waited for me," Deka said darkly. The nerve of not having a committee to welcome still rankled his princess.

"We kind of had other shit to deal with. Like, you know, the apocalypse and all."

"What has the suzerain done?"

"Who?" Babette blinked at him.

"Freaky, red-eyed chick, sometimes a dude, wants to rule the world?" Deka explained.

"Oh, her. She's going by the name Voa, Boa, something or other. And she's been popping up all over the place with her minions of annoyance."

"Has she stated what she wants?"

"World domination." The duh tone said it all.

"How big is her army?"

Babette shrugged. "Hard to tell because they often attack in small groups in multiple places at once. And it's not just dragons she's subverted fighting for her. She's got humans, and even some of the other cryptos battling under her banner. Which, oddly enough, is a dragon with squiggles coming out of it."

"Because she's a dragon," Samael admitted, more than a little grimly.

"Bullshit!" Babette exclaimed. "But she doesn't look like a dragon. And I hear she doesn't smell like one either."

"Suzie's got all kinds of talents, including eating souls to get stronger."

"Okay, that's just wrong."

"Exactly, and we have to stop her," Deka declared.

"We?" Samael shot her a look.

"Yes, we. Team..." Deka paused. "We need a cool name."

"No," he stated. "We don't—"

As if they'd let him finish that thought.

"How about Team Sausage and Buns?"

"No, that's too foody. We need something elegant but dangerous." Deka tapped her chin. "The Rampaging Duo."

Babette scrunched up her face. "But then that implies I can't come along sometimes for fun."

"Trio?"

Again, Babette shook her head. "Then people will think we're in a ménage. My girlfriend wouldn't like that."

"You're dating?" Deka squealed. "Who is it?"

"You don't know her. I met her in Paris," Babette confided, a pink blush to her cheeks.

"That is amazing, cuz. I want to hear all the details."

"Can we get back to the end of the world?" he barked.

"No." It came in stereo, and he scowled.

"I'm going to have a shower." He turned around and began stalking through his castle, only to have a body launch itself at his back and hold on.

"Mind if I join you? Who are we both kidding? We both know you'd love it if I came along."

"Your friend invaded my castle." He still hadn't quite gotten over that fact, that and the threat that more might be coming.

"Get used to being barged in on. My family has few boundaries."

"I like my privacy."

"No one says you can't still like it, but you will have less of it now that you have me. I think I might be a slight bit possessive."

He reached over and dragged her off his back into his arms. "I am, too, which is why the idea of sharing you with a bunch of people is annoying."

"But you'll put up with it for me."

"Yes." Grudgingly said. "For now. However, don't get used to it. I intend to tighten security."

"Good luck with that. My aunts are the best in the biz. They'll think it's fun to crack it."

"I can't even believe we're discussing this. Shouldn't we be more worried about the fact that Suzie is trying to take over the world?"

"Oh, please. Like that will ever happen. The dragons might be slow-moving when it comes to some things, but once the decision is made, we'll fight back. I think."

"What do you mean, think? Wasn't that why we returned?"

"Well, yeah, we'll definitely go and tackle her ass, but I can't talk for the Septs."

"Not even the Silver one?"

She shook her head. "They will follow the ruling of the king."

"And if my brother decides to not get

involved?"

She shrugged. "Then Suzie might be able to do some damage, and he won't have much left to rule. But it won't come to that because we won't let her ruin our world. Right?"

Her confidence was misplaced. What did one half-breed Golden have that was so special?

He looked down at the silver head nestled against his chest.

I have a reason to not lose.

His bedroom was in the topmost tower or, as Deka declared with a clap of her hands, "Penthouse suite. Nice, muffin."

Nicer was the giant-size bed with a real mattress and clean sheets. Nicest of all? The bathroom with all the hot water and shower jets a person could ask for.

"Last one in is a rotten wyvern egg."

"Wyverns don't have eggs," he retorted. But he had to smile as she ditched her clothes, revealing that perfect body of hers, which looked much better wrapped around his.

She dove into the shower and squealed as she turned the knob and cold water initially shot out. She laughed, the crystal-clear sound the most precious thing he'd ever heard.

So many things about her were precious.

And mine.

Mustn't forget that. He didn't know if it was because she kept insisting or if he was finally ready to admit it, but they belonged together.

He needed her.

Needed her right now.

The face she turned up to him as he towered over her held a smile and a hint of erotic promise.

"Hey, stud muffin. Is that for me?" She would have grabbed his erection, but he caught her first, gripping her hands in his fists, dragging them down to her sides. It drew her tight against him, so tight, they were skin-to-skin, naked flesh that trembled at the contact.

A languorous look shuttered her eyes as she stared at him. Unlike other women, she wasn't intimidated at all. Nor did he see the avarice that often tainted the gazes of those who knew who and what he was. Nothing but desire shone in her depths.

A desire reciprocated.

The longer he stared, the more her lids drooped, and her gaze dropped to his mouth.

Kiss me.

She demanded, and he was more than happy to comply. He dipped his head that he might claim her lips. Arousal coursed through him, fierce and fast. The taste of her boiled his blood.

His hands skimmed over her frame, stroking her flesh, reacquainting himself and, at the same time, reclaiming what was his.

Because you are mine.

She heard him and laughed against his lips. *All yours, stud. I am never leaving.*

Where once he might have seen those words as a threat, he now recognized them for a promise, a bond that only grew stronger between them.

I should claim you. Here. Now.

Except she thought, *No.*

He pulled back. "What do you mean, no?"

Despite their lips having parted, she clutched at his shoulders, fingers digging into his flesh, attempting to draw him back.

"Not no as in we'll never do it. No as in not

right now. I want you. Don't doubt that. But when I put my mark on you, it will be in front of an audience because I don't want any doubt that I chose you, and I want everyone to know."

His nostrils flared as his emotions tumbled, so many of them at once, but the most prevalent?

Satisfaction. *You are mine.* And she was right. When he claimed her, and that was no longer even a question, he would do so in a way that left no doubt as to that fact.

Deft fingers stroked her bare skin, reveling in the silky smoothness, finding her ticklish spots just because he liked to hear her giggle.

Her soft laughter tickled his mouth, and he swallowed it, swallowed every sweet sound she made in his arms. She also stroked him, but she wasn't gentle about her touch, gripping him, digging her nails in, passion giving her strength. The urgency of her need caressed him as surely as her skin did rubbing against his, the water of the shower making them slick.

His eager cock found itself trapped between their bodies, pulsing against her lower belly. The bed sat only a few yards away, too far and too drafty for their wet bodies.

Why leave the hot, steamy shower when it was large enough for what he had planned? Cupping her ass, his hands filled with her full cheeks, he raised her, and she didn't need to be told to wrap her legs around his waist. The heat of her core pressed against his skin. Pulsed.

He shifted her enough that his cock sprang free and bounced under her butt. He then lowered her enough to seesaw it against her wet slit. A most glorious moan slipped from her, the kind that shivered through the body.

Sexiest fucking thing ever.

He aimed the swollen tip of his shaft at her sex, pressing it lightly against her damp lips. It took only the slightest pressure to penetrate, the walls of her cunt squeezing him.

Yes.

The mental voice, him or her, it didn't matter. He hissed as her head tilted.

He slid balls-deep into her and sat there, slightly grinding himself into her, a swirl and push of his hips that drove him deep.

She stuttered. "Oh, damn. Damn." Her fingers dug into his back, sharp and strong. As strong as the grip she had on him.

"That's it, princess." *My queen.*

Damned straight.

The intimate connection of their minds kept blowing him away. There was no mistaking who she was in his head. She existed as part of him and somehow enhanced every experience.

I can feel your enjoyment, he thought, feel how complicated her emotions were about him, but in a good way.

She truly does want me.

Of course, I do, stud.

Because they belonged together. He thrust into her, keeping her back pressed against the shower wall, his hips pistoning.

"Harder," she panted.

He couldn't. He'd hurt her.

Give it to me. The words growled into his mind.

She commanded, and he couldn't help but obey.

He thrust harder, in and out, the friction slick.

But it wasn't enough for her.

She needed something more.

He manhandled her, pulling her down, ignoring her mewl of protest that he might stand her facing the wall. A hand curled around her thigh and pulled her ass back toward him.

His other hand stroked the round cheek. "Spread your legs."

She kicked them apart and thrust her ass out a little bit more. The perfect height for him to slam his cock back in.

She cried out as he pumped in and out, but he got her to come hard when he slipped a hand under and began to finger her clit.

She rippled around him, her channel pulsing in time to her orgasm. It was incredible, especially when you added in the fact that he felt her come, like *felt* it.

No wonder she liked it so much.

He came, possibly twice, because she said, *I love you.*

Chapter Nineteen

Oh, shit. I said it first. Deka slammed a door on her mind and tried to shut off any hint of what she'd just said.

Maybe he didn't hear me.

Was it a bad thing if he had?

Well, yeah, it's bad. I said it first!

It smacked of desperation. Deka didn't do desperate.

He kissed the top of her head as he leaned against her, his cock still sheathed.

Fuck, that was good sex.

Like really good sex. The kind that had her hungry pussy begging for round two.

But first more soap, then food.

Then sex.

Lots of sex. She opened her mind to let him catch a glimpse of her plan.

She got her second orgasm before the food, in bed.

And a third with dessert.

At this point, she was half dead. Her pussy literally purring worse than any cat and happier than she'd ever been where she lay sprawled atop him.

Her fingers lazily circled his nipple. A nice nipple. She'd claimed it with a nibble a few times. Licked it, too.

It now belonged to her, along with his cock.

That nice dick is so mine. Best dick ever.

Like, seriously, there should be an award because he'd so win it.

As for his nipple, it would achieve perfection once it had a nipple ring. Just one to give him a pirate look.

What about a cock ring... She peeked down at his shaft.

The chest under her cheek rumbled. "I am not getting any piercings."

He read her mind with an ease that pleased her. The bond between them grew, even if part of him still hesitated.

Or maybe he doesn't feel it. After all, he'd not said anything after her accidental "I love you."

"Think of the fun I'd have with a piercing down there." She nipped his chin.

"I think we already have plenty of fun without it."

"True. I like the fun." And she liked Samael. A lot. And not just because he was a Golden prize or a good lay or cute.

She liked him, even his strange quirks.

"I am not strange."

"Yeah, you are, but so am I, so that makes it cool."

She blew hotly against his chest and listened to the steady thump of his heart speed up. And the faint echo of a second heart. How fascinating.

"What's fascinating?"

"The way you're changing."

He froze. "It's not exactly easy to admit."

"Let me help. Yes, I have two heartbeats, and some horns, but I'm still a very hot stud." Even if he was the only dragon to ever have horns. Well, except for old paintings, but those were surely exaggerated.

"Horns?" He sounded startled. "I don't have fucking horns."

"If you say so."

"What are you saying?"

Since he seemed a little perturbed, she tucked her hands behind her back and said a very convincingly long, "Nu-u-h-thing."

"Deka!"

"Forget I said it. Totally wrong person and thing to say. What did you mean when you admitted you were changing?"

"I was talking about the fact you're turning me into some oddly possessive and mushy pathetic worm who wants to worship you and kill anyone who looks your way."

"That's not change, muffin, that's fate. And I have no problem with you having a jealous fit." Kind of sexy, actually.

"You're not helping. I want to go back to the horns. Did you seriously see some?" He copped a feel of his forehead, which appeared smooth—for the moment.

She tugged his hands away from his head. "Forget the horns."

"I can't. You obviously saw some. What the fuck does it mean? Am I a freak?"

"You're not a freak, and since you insist on knowing, they're devilishly attractive and only visible when you're a dragon. And I'm sure they won't get much larger."

He cringed. "How big are they?"

"Hard to tell since they began spiraling."

"Princess!" The warning tone made her roll

her eyes.

"Stop the whining already. So what if you're not the same as other dragons? Instead of freaking out about it, celebrate it."

"Celebrate the fact that I'm a mutant?"

"Think of it more as transitioning to a new state."

"But why is this happening? Why now?"

She shrugged. "Dunno, but if I had to guess, I'd say the time we spent in that hell zone drew out that other side of you."

"What side, though? Do you think this has to do with my father?"

"Probably. We never did figure out what he was."

"It might be important."

"How? It won't change anything. You are who you are."

"What if he's alive?"

"What if he just donated sperm and never could be bothered to find out if it took root? Maybe he's an asshole who goes around making babies and abandoning them and deserves a kick in the head for not being there when you were growing up."

Perhaps the psychiatrist she'd sent to the loony bin by scaring her with her real face might have had a point. Deka might have some deep-seated daddy issues about her own birth.

"You make it sound easy."

"Because it is."

"Yet you have no idea what it's like for me. I went from top of the world to…"

"To what? Hot stud muffin lucky enough to snare the most incredible woman in the universe?"

His lips curved into an insanely sweet smile, a

smile just for her. "You are incredible. And beautiful. And a shit ton of other things. While I'm a mixed-gene freak with nothing to offer but this castle underground."

"The castle is pretty sweet."

He growled.

"But even if you didn't have a single penny to your name, I'd still want you. You're pretty damned awesome, muffin. And since I am the center of everything, and have declared it, it's time you accepted it. Say it. I am Deka's awesome stud muffin."

"Like fuck."

"There you go with that pessimism again. I thought we talked about that being forbidden. Hold on." She sat up in the bed, tits projecting nicely, hair a jumbled mess, and said, "I hereby declare that your negative attitude be banished."

"It's not that easy."

"It is if I declare it."

He shook his head but smiled. "You're something else."

"I know. Deal with it."

"So, now what?"

"We get wild again?" She waggled her brows and smiled suggestively.

"Maybe after some food. I mean, what's the next step?"

"Ass-kicking and saving the world."

He sighed. "I meant for you and me. Where do we go from here?"

"I'd say it's obvious. You just need to say the words." Because she'd already made her intent very clear. But even she had some pride. The next move was up to him.

"Deka, I—" Whatever romantic declaration he would have made—and it would have been epic because, hello, the man was so obviously in love with her—was interrupted by a heifer who was instantly demoted from her best friend position. When Deka became queen someday—because she didn't think small—she'd outlaw cock-blocking.

Babette, though, with no regard for true friendship, barged in yelling, "Incoming!"

Chapter Twenty

Invasion!

Dammit. From secret hideaway to sudden hot spot. Apparently, his hidden home was no longer safe.

Samael threw on a pair of pants the moment he rolled out of bed. It took him but a few steps to hit a security console and key up the active cameras. It didn't take long to find the problem.

An intruder had discovered his secret entry, the one by the river, accessible only to someone who could fly with a keen eye for detail—and who didn't mind a bit of bat shit.

Then, if you got past that, there was the second underwater tunnel, tight to fit through, the chamber of spiders, always guaranteed to make people scream, and then, if they managed to top that, the shiny room. Lots of pretty, shiny things to draw the avarice-eyed. When they slowed, bam, incinerated with napalm.

A brilliant defense system that wouldn't stop the person coming.

I don't have much time.

He turned and saw that Deka sat on the bed, naked and gorgeous. Soft and vulnerable.

"Stay here," he ordered.

She arched a brow. "I'm coming with you."

"No, you're not." He strode quickly to the door and slammed it shut, then locked it. For her own safety, which was why he didn't understand the litany of names she called him as she pounded on it.

Probably relief under the shrieking anger that he was being so thoughtful about her wellbeing.

Knowing he'd have to face this invader—*I can't hide from this*—Samael stood on the smoothed plane of stone that acted as the courtyard to his castle.

Around him, the crash of water as it tumbled into the crystal-lined pond masked most sound, and yet he felt him coming.

My nemesis. His biggest regret.

Through the tunnel bored through stone from centuries of flow, his brother emerged, shooting into the cavern, a golden streak that, for the moment, blinded as the ambient lighting reflected off the shiny scales.

A big, healthy, and power-oozing dragon, it appeared Remiel had taken well to kinghood.

Samael, on the other hand, was having issues. And he wasn't talking about the horns he'd yet to see. He'd not mentioned it to Deka, but he'd noticed changes, too.

He knew about the second heartbeat, the strange tingle inside him, and odder glimpses of another world. A layer to this one with the most bizarre glowing lights.

Weird shit, but the most worrisome, the zaps of power—*it's magic, say it.* He wanted to deny what happened. Magic was supposed to be fun. Singeing his ass when wiping wasn't his idea of a good time.

Neither were the random jolts of power that had shattered his morning cup of coffee while in Hell.

He'd even zinged Deka a few times when they

fucked. Although that meant her pussy squeezed him so tightly he just about burst. So that zap, he didn't mind.

But it made him wonder, *What's wrong with me?* Would Remiel see the sickness within and seek to destroy it before it spread?

Holding himself aloft on his mighty wings, Remiel trumpeted a greeting. *There you are!*

"I see your powers of observation are keen," was Samael's sarcastic reply.

Just as rude as ever. The blaring bugle was a warning to ready himself for battle.

"Must we?" he said with a sigh. He'd left a warm bed and an even hotter naked body for this?

With only the slightest of effort, he turned into his dragon self, and made the mistake, as he towered taller than before, of peeking at his reflection in the water. Even distorted, he couldn't miss the protrusions on his forehead.

Fuck me, there they are. Curling, black horns. He would have touched them, but dragons, much like a T-rex, couldn't rub their heads—either of them. It probably explained their anger issues.

What's that sticking out of your head? Remiel mind-spoke to him.

Usually only mates could speak mind to mind, however it was recently discovered to be a trait of a Golden king that he might order his armies when not in human form.

A fashion statement, Samael thought back to his hovering brother.

Since when do you have horns?

Samael shrugged. Some things just didn't have a reply.

What have you been up to?

Did he really want to get into the whole capture and torture by a crazy chick? Dick? Whatever.

No.

Plotting to take your throne, while not the most conducive to his health answer, totally gave him the biggest balls of them all.

Remiel burst with sound, and Samael braced himself for the attack. Surely, Remiel would try to kill him. After everything Samael had done...

Instead of attacking, Remiel drifted down, tucked his wings, and sat. He also stared.

Two could play at casual cool. Samael crossed his arms. Again, not far, the short-limb-versus-wide-chest thing.

When nothing was said for a long moment, he finally cracked and uttered a trilling note. *Why are you here?*

He received a trumpet in reply. *Does a brother need a reason to visit?*

If he'd had regular eyelids, Samael might have blinked. *You hate me.*

Not as much as I used to.

Okay. That made no sense. *I helped keep you prisoner.*

You didn't have much choice.

I should have tried to fight Parker. But I didn't.

Because you are an idiot.

At that, Samael blarted and shifted back to man. "I am not an idiot."

"How else," Remiel asked, shifting as well, their resemblance despite their different fathers uncanny, "do you explain getting caught by a witch?"

He wouldn't ask how Remiel knew about his capture by the suzerain. A king should be well informed.

"It was a sorceress, thank you very much, one so powerful she was banished eons ago."

"So I heard. She's been whining about it on national television. Someone needs to get over it."

It kind of mirrored his thoughts. "She's a nutjob."

"She is, and now, thanks to you, is out there roaming the world causing all kinds of trouble."

"You're blaming me for this?" Samael bristled. "I had nothing to fucking do with it. She was a psycho before she escaped her hell prison."

"Why didn't you stop her?"

"What part of I was her prisoner did you not get?"

"The part where you were a prisoner. Pathetic, dude."

He blinked. For real this time. "Dude? Did we suddenly become teenagers at the fucking beach?"

"What else would you like me to call you? Brother? I'm not quite ready for that. Asshole seems like a rather counterproductive way to rebuild our relationship."

"What relationship? I was an asshole. You should hate me." He didn't say it for pity or forgiveness. It was fact. Samael had come to terms with his actions. If given another chance…he'd probably repeat them in the hopes of being king.

Remiel appeared sad. "I would have let you have the title. You know I never wanted the throne."

"You seem to be enjoying it now. *King.*" He couldn't stop the sneer.

"Parker and Anastasia didn't leave me much choice." Remiel shrugged his broad shoulders. "It's not as bad as expected. It comes with perks, such as bossing people around. A nice change from our youth, eh?"

"I wouldn't know. I never really got a chance to be the boss. People were always trying to tell me what to do."

"Yet you found ways to do your own thing." Remiel gestured to the cavern. "This wasn't Anastasia's or Parker's doing."

"A castle isn't a big accomplishment."

"Take pride in the things you did, not the things you didn't," Remiel uttered with a sageness greater than his years. "Holding on to the past, and the would-have, could-have, should-have moments doesn't help you move forward into the future."

"Pretending it didn't happen doesn't make it go away. I did bad things. People won't forget."

"They'll have to if I order them." Remiel's lips ghosted into a smile, and Samael couldn't help but frown.

"And what of the fact that I was dating Sue-Ellen for a while? Are you ready to forgive and forget that?"

At that, Remiel's eyes flashed gold. "The fact that it never went further than a few kisses is the only reason you're alive."

Magnanimous of his brother, especially considering Samael was going to have to have a talk with Deka, complete with a pen and paper so he could make a list of the males who would have to disappear. He feared the list might be rather lengthy.

His woman had a lusty appetite.

But from now on, she would eat only him.

"If you're not here to kill me, then why are you here?"

"Hoping you have a cold beer in that hidden fortress of yours."

"You and I don't do that kind of shit." Normal families did. They were far from normal. "What do you want from me?" Did Remiel want his head? An apology on his knees? Was this simply a buttering-up moment before Remiel went all Golden bad-ass and decapitated him?

"What do you think I should demand from the only blood family I have? The one who betrayed me? The one who was just as sorely abused? Do you want to die by my hand?"

"Don't you dare kill him."

No surprise, a locked room couldn't hold her. Deka came flying out of his castle, wearing a shirt of his and not much else. She looked wickedly sexy, completely unhinged, and about to commit regicide— which probably wouldn't go over well.

Samael snared her before she could plunge her nails into Remiel and start something he didn't want to finish.

"Stop," Samael said.

I won't let him touch you.

He's your king. You should obey.

As if. You could be king. She hissed in his mind.

Not at the expense of his brother.

Funny how it took him this long to realize some things cost too much.

She kicked and screamed in his grip, a rabid dragoness protecting her man. "Let me at him, muffin. I don't care who he is. We'll bury the body somewhere no one will find it. I won't let him hurt you."

The sentiment gave him warm and fuzzy heartburn.

Remiel arched a brow. "As deranged as ever, I see."

"It's one of her more endearing traits," Samael said through gritted teeth as he locked his arms around her.

Deka snarled. "I won't let you take him from me. King or not. He's mine."

"Calm yourself. You can have him. But first, he has to do something for me. For the world, actually." Remiel faced him, his expression quite serious. "You wanted to know why I came. I'll admit, it's a selfish reason. I need you to help me."

He frowned. "Help you? How?"

"You're the only one who can do anything against Voadicia."

The name caused his brows to rise. "Are you out of your fucking mind? I can't help. I didn't beat her. She held me prisoner."

"You got out."

"Only because princess here found a way." The shame burned, but not as much as the fact that his brother thought Samael had something to offer. How wrong he was.

Of a sudden, the world's smallest violin played a sad, sad song in his head, followed by a distinct snicker as Deka said, *Don't be such a prima donna. Or are you trying to have someone stroke your ego? Man up.*

He wanted to, but... He shook his head.

Slap. Deka had slipped from his grip and stood in front of him. "What did I say about the woe is me stuff?"

Had she seriously slapped him?

He glared at her. "Hitting isn't nice."

"I tried using my words, and then you pissed me off. And are you seriously complaining about a girl slapping you?"

"You are more than a girl, and you hit hard."

"But it worked. You're not acting like some puny pussy, lying down and being all dramatic like. Oh, no, I can't do this. I'm not good enough, blah blah blah. You want to claim you're a loser? Do that after you at least try."

He glared at her. "And if I'm right and I fail?"

"Then we will give you a hero's burial."

"As pep talks go, that one rather sucked."

"Do you need another slap?"

"You do realize my brother is asking me to do the impossible," Samael noted.

"How do you know it's impossible? Have you truly thought about it? Besides, I thought you wanted to fight."

"I do. On my terms." He glared at his brother. He dropped his voice and leaned toward Deka. *I don't want him banking everything on me. What if I fail?*

You won't, was her soft reply.

Aloud, Remiel said, "Believe in yourself. You have to believe because, without you, I fear we are doomed. You and you alone have magic to counter hers."

At that, Samael laughed. "Magic? What the hell did you sniff? I don't have magic."

It might explain what's happening to you.

Remiel fixed him with a stare. "Stop denying it. You know what I'm saying is true. I wasn't sure until I saw you."

"And what do you see?" Samael turned in a circle. "No beard. No long robes. Not even a proper staff. Exactly what makes you think I'm a wizard?"

"Because, according to the hidden history books I've read, only dragons who can wield magic grow horns."

Chapter Twenty-one

Poor Sammy. He almost fainted. Mostly because he started laughing so hard that he ran out of breath.

But the mirth was just a front. As soon as Remiel left, he'd marched off to the bedroom, dragging her with him, muttering, "I'm not a fucking wizard."

Someone was in denial.

Someone was also wearing too much clothing.

Take it off. You know you want to. No matter how subtly, and not so subtly, she suggested he strip, he remained partially clothed.

At least she'd gotten frustrated sex—which was the fast and furious kind for the curious—before he started pacing, his sexy body covered in a terry cloth bathrobe that did more to enhance his yumminess than hide it. Less yummy was the doubt he kept displaying. It kept overriding his excitement at Remiel's revelation.

"A wizard?" he muttered for the umpteenth time.

"I think it's rather cool." Other heifers had plain old dragons or wyverns for boyfriends. She had a freaking sorcerer. Baboom!

"I don't like it."

"Why?" Because, personally, all she could see were the infinite possibilities.

"Because now Remiel is expecting shit from me. Everyone is. They're out of their minds."

"I don't see why you're freaking. You have magic."

"I have it, but I don't know how to use it." He whirled to stare at her, his eyes wide, the arrogance stifled under panic. "How am I supposed to learn magic? There are no books. No teachers. No one to show me what the fuck I'm supposed to do."

"How hard can it be?" Of course, when she said it, she might have been staring below his waist.

He glared. He did it quite well. Royally even, his aquiline features perfectly made for regal glaring. "Can you keep your attention off my cock for five minutes?"

"No."

"Stop making me horny. This is serious," he yelled.

"So is my need for your cock."

"You can have my cock after you help me figure out how I can wield magic against a centuries-old witch and win."

"Practice lobbing some powerballs at dummies and then, in the final battle, knock her out. Problem solved. Now, bring me my prize."

He didn't budge. "I might not know much about magic, but I am pretty sure it requires more than five minutes of practice."

"Says the guy who hasn't even tried." She sighed. Obviously, there would be no sex until she helped him. "Have you searched YouTube to see if anyone posted any videos?" Given his silence, she would guess no. "If we can't find any, then we could always see what's on Netflix."

"How is that supposed to teach me anything?"

he roared.

"It doesn't, but it would be less boring than this conversation. You're a wizard. Do wizardly things. Like that dude in the walking tree movie."

He growled. "Do I look like Gandalf?

"Grow out a beard, and I'll let you know."

"This isn't funny, princess."

"Never said it was. You're the one being all drama king about it. I was being very serious. I am willing to wager my mint-condition Wonder Woman figurine that you'd rock a beard. Just think, I could yank on it during sex, you could tickle my clit with it." When he continued to scowl, she sighed. "Why are you so convinced you can't learn to do magic?"

"Because I haven't the slightest clue where to start."

"But you know two guys who do."

He blinked. "What are you talking about? I don't know any wizards."

"Yeah, you do. Think about it." Just in case he needed a hint, she began to hum the theme song from *Star Wars*.

It took him a second before his eyes got that light bulb moment. "The Jabbas."

"Ding ding ding. Give the man a prize." She flung herself on the bed, arms and legs akimbo, waiting for him to claim it, but instead, he continued to pace, hand rubbing his chin.

"They are part of the original group of wizards banished all those centuries ago, but will they help me? I did lock them up. And then left."

"So, you set them free."

"Is that wise, though?"

"You're the wizard; you tell me."

He snorted. "I don't feel very wizardly."

"Says the man who makes me feel magic every time he touches me."

For a moment, his eyes turned smoky. "What if they lead me astray? Or won't teach me?"

"Won't?" She arched a brow. "Do I have to remind you again who you are?"

"You're right." He stood tall, broad, deadly. "I am Samael D'Ore, a direct descendent of the Golden line, not a hybrid experiment. They will teach me or face my wrath." He punched the palm of his hand with a fist.

So hot.

"That's my stud muffin. Now come here and thank me for solving your problem."

"Why don't you come here and thank me?"

Curiosity had her cocking her head and saying, "For what?"

"Because I'm about to make you come so hard you'll go cross-eyed."

And he did. He also had her screaming his name and clawing his back.

Then he left, without her, to go visit the Jabbas, taking no one with him.

Ditched his princess for his brother, but she was okay with that. He was a man on a mission while she was a woman with an ever-increasing posse of curious dragonesses who kept popping in and not leaving.

Who knew the pic she posted on Instagram would go viral among the Septs? Who knew so many would come flocking to the Underground Lair of Deviousness—as she'd nicknamed it.

Who knew how much she'd miss Samael once he'd been gone for a few days.

I should have gone with him.

But Samael was right when he claimed she would be a distraction—*I can't think straight when you're around on account that all the blood rushes to my dick. If you want to have that claiming ceremony, then you'll obey me and stay behind.*

She didn't do it to obey. Hell, no. She made the ultimate sacrifice and let him go off alone to become a super wizard because hello, more power!

In the meantime, with him gone—but surely thinking of her every single second—Deka took the liberty of redecorating a few rooms.

I'm sure he'll love it. Especially the pink flamingoes she'd had brought in for his pond. They added a festive flair, as did the patio lanterns.

However, between the shopping, and occasional skirmish—because, hello, war on Earth meant good times fighting—she moped.

Funny thing she discovered, while the world revolved around her, despite what those other heifers thought, it turned out her happiness revolved around him.

About ten days after he'd left—during which a menstrual period sadly came and went meaning no bun in the oven—she wandered into the war room. Previously known as his office, now taken over and also redecorated—because the addition of a *Star Trek* theme just made it that much more badass.

She entered, wearing black again, to hear, "Look, it's Princess Mopey," announced by Sheila. That bitch. She'd arrived with her husband and kids last week and set up camp aboveground in the farmhouse—which, as it turned out, was more solid than it looked. She was now acting as the doorman to the farmhouse entrance, and her kids were freaking out new arrivals by silently exiting the fields and staring.

"I am not moping," Deka said before tucking her lip back in.

"Are you here to check on the plans for the final battle?" asked her mother. Mommy Dearest had arrived hours after Samael left. Took one look at her watery eyes—because this castle was damned dusty—and proceeded to make Deka cookies. By the dozens. Mother always knew how to cheer her up.

But now, she wouldn't leave. Apparently, Australia was one of the places they figured the final battle would occur. Britain was another, as was Maysville, Kentucky. Don't ask why the precision; every one of the seers said it.

If Deka had a say, the final battle would be on the beach so they could all go for a swim after. The best part was, then the blood would attract sharks and they'd have plenty to eat for the barbecue afterwards.

But no one would listen to her. Nope, they were going off some old prophecies and tracking Suzie's troop movements and other boring, rational stuff.

Given they couldn't predict the exact location of the battle, the Septs had split up to ensure they were represented in all the likely spots. That meant Deka got Mommy butting in, along with a few other Silvers. But it wasn't just the Silvers converging on her lair.

The other colored Septs were contributing, too. Especially the Aussie-based ones, who didn't want the Americans homing in on their turf. She did enjoy her Down Under cousins, though. They knew how to get bulk loads of Tim Tams.

Snacks were super important at this stage of the conflict. Tensions were high, and with this many women in one spot, it meant Samael's office now sported quite a few bowls and other stashes of candy and chocolate—because no one wanted to deal with a PMSing dragoness in need of sugar.

"Where's Voa at now?" Since only Samael understood why she used the nickname Suzie, Deka had had to adopt the more commonly accepted name for the suzerain.

"She just rammed through the wall of China and unleashed some ancient stone army."

"Have we sent any help?" Deka asked, plopping her butt in the high heel chair with its plush, pink velvet fabric.

"Are you nuts? You know the Chinese dragons don't like anyone coming in on their turf."

Unfortunately, their Asian counterparts had yet to realize they'd need to stand together if they were to prevail. They needed to make a strong showing, all of them together, if they wanted to push Voa back.

They also needed magic to fight magic because the longer Voa was on Earth, the stronger she got.

Someone's been gorging on souls. One had to wonder how she didn't get fat.

And how long before she ate so many she became invincible?

Where are you, Samael? We need you.

They'd heard nothing since he left.

No love note for Deka. No sexy pic for her to masturbate with. Nothing but the faint feeling of him, far away, but still living. Hopefully, learning magic. But would those lessons be enough? Would Samael return in time for the coming battle?

Doubt had no place in her life, so Deka chose to ignore it. They would win. Because she said so.

And because she'd yet to claim her stubborn muffin.

Elspeth bounced in, blond curls jiggling, her cheerful smile causing more than a few groans. "Hello, everyone. What a wonderful day." Every day was wonderful to the always-happy Elspeth. Her bubbly nature and happy disposition made more than a few of them draw fingers across their throats.

The damned canary-yellow dragoness was happiness personified. Nothing ever brought her down. Everything was sunshine and rainbows. Glass half full. And all that crap.

She didn't have an arrogant, greedy bone in her body. Her mother must have been so ashamed of her child's infirmity.

"Isn't there a rock in need of a pep talk in the garden?" someone asked.

"I already told them one day they'd become diamonds, they just needed to be patient." Surely, that was madness and not genuine glee in her shining eyes?

"You do realize the end of the world is coming?" snapped Babette, who seemed more surly than usual.

Elspeth clapped her hands and rocked on her heels, smiling so widely, surely her head would split. "Is it the end, or just a new beginning? What if the coming battle means a better world for everyone?"

Groans abounded.

Babette loudest of all. "I doubt it. Everything sucks."

"Oh, poor Babsy. Don't be so grumpy." Elspeth dove on Babette and lifted her off her feet in an enthusiastic hug—at six feet plus, the girl wasn't dainty. "Everything will work out just fine. Just because your girlfriend has been ignoring you doesn't mean you're not loved."

"What do you mean that bitch is ignoring you?" Deka interjected. This was the first she'd heard of Babette having issues with her new girlfriend. "Want me to beat her up?" Because she wanted to hit something, and she couldn't slap Elspeth around. One didn't hurt the arrogantly challenged.

"It's nothing," Babette muttered. "I mean, the apocalypse is coming. She's probably busy."

"Too busy for you? I don't think so." Deka latched on to the travesty of ignoring her very bestest friend. "Let's call that no-good ho right now."

"She's not a ho. I'm sure she has a good reason."

"When was the last time you talked?"

Babette shrugged, lips downturned. "Yesterday. She hung up on me, like midsentence. Which was weird, 'cause we weren't arguing or nothing. Just talking about the war and what we were doing to help it."

"She's a dragon?" someone asked from across the room.

Babette's brow creased. "I don't know."

"What do you mean, you don't know?" asked Deka's mother, who lifted her head from a stack of reports. "Is she human? Because, if she is, then you shouldn't be discussing the conflict at all."

"But the humans know about the war." They couldn't exactly miss it, given that their cities were burning.

"Humans shouldn't be privy to dragon news. So"—Xylia turned on Babette—"what is she?"

"She's—I—" Babette's face creased, and she couldn't seem to talk. Probably overwrought by the ho who'd ditched her coldly.

Deka hated seeing her like this. And she needed something to do. "Let's call her."

Over Babette's protest, her cell phone was snared, hooked up to the screen suspended on the wall, and a Skype call was placed.

The phone rang. *Ring. Ring.* Went to a generic voicemail box that recited a short "leave a message" in a computer monotone.

"She's not answering," Babette said with a shrug.

"More like she didn't want to. That's the message you get when someone intentionally ignores a call," Sheila remarked as she tapped a few keys.

As if that was allowed. Deka rose from her slipper shoe throne. "Someone hack that phone and get it to accept the call."

In short order, the phone rang again, and through the magic of modern technology, on the big screen, a room appeared.

A war room much like the one they were in, except for one thing.

"Holy shit, Babette. Voa kidnapped your girlfriend and stole her phone." At Deka's shout, Voa turned around, her bright red eyes fixing on the cell phone screen.

"What do you want?" snapped the sorceress. "I'm kind of busy taking over the world."

"Not for long, bitch. I'm coming for you. If you want a quick death, though, hand over Babette's girlfriend."

The eyes flared brightly for a moment, and Voa's face came uncomfortably close to the screen. Not her best look, given the size of her nostrils. "You're worried about Suzanne." The smile proved much too wide.

For a being that could change shape, you'd figure she'd be more attractive.

"Where is she?" Babette stood in front of the screen, fists clenched. "You'd better not have harmed her."

"Your girlfriend is fine. As a matter of fact…" Voa's face darkened, and at first, Deka thought they were losing the connection, only the face morphed and the hair shifted and…

"Suzanne?" Babette's tremulous query cemented the deal.

"Holy smokes, cuz, you were sleeping with the enemy." And probably spilling secrets. That, and hopefully not a surprise lesbian pregnancy, was why Babette went running for a garbage can and threw up.

Deka glared at the screen. "How dare you break Babette's heart!"

"All's fair in war. She gave me what I needed. Just like you will all feed me what I need when I come for you."

"Never." The word came from behind her, and not from just any man, *her* man, dressed to the nines in head-to-toe black and looking so badass, Deka creamed her panties and then punched the woman beside her for doing the same.

"Stud muffin, you're home!" Deka exclaimed, but he only spared her a quick, smoldering glance before facing the screen.

"Your reign of terror is going to end," he declared.

Voa laughed. "It's only just begun."

"My boyfriend is going to kick your ass," Deka declared. "Because he's awesome."

"I guess we'll soon see. The battle will be in three days."

"Make that forty-eight hours," Samael corrected. "I've got a wedding to attend."

"Who's getting married?" she asked.

"We are."

Good thing he was steady on his feet because her flying leap might have had a little more oomph than expected.

Chapter Twenty-two

Hours later, in bed, naked, and...*I could totally go for a smoke*, Deka sighed—because, yeah, the sex was that good—and uttered, "Show me."

"I thought I just did." He couldn't help a smile.

She matched it and took it up a level with, "Your grins should come with a warning. Mini orgasm ahead. Now, stop stalling and show me."

"Show you what?"

"Your magic, stud. Dazzle me," Deka demanded as she lounged on his bed wearing nothing but his scent. It suited her. Suited her very well.

The urge to mark her now, before the battle, was strong. So strong. His need for her was never clearer than during the time he'd spent apart from her.

He worried about her every second. Missed her something fierce.

And yet he used those emotions to focus on his lessons with the Jabba brothers. The sooner he mastered his new skills, the sooner he could return to her side.

Now, he had to prepare for the biggest event of his life.

His wedding.

Because he wasn't worried about the fight. He

had a plan. An epic one. A strategy he would invoke in two days.

Two days of furious preparation by the dragons and their allies. Messages flew, as did people, all of them wanting to be part of the battle.

The final stage was set to happen in the Great Victoria Desert, the largest desert in Australia, the perfect stage for the upcoming festivities.

The clock ticked down. Everyone of import was aware of the epic event happening. Everyone wanted to be present and had done their utmost to look his or her best.

Standing on the reddish-orange sand as dawn crested and lit the world on fire, he tried not to fidget or sweat in his robes—not a dress.

If you say so, muffin.

Samael stood at Remiel's right side, a position of honor accorded to him by the brother he'd wronged.

A chance for redemption.

And power, muffin. Don't forget the power.

He hadn't. He might not wear the mantle of king, let his brother bear that heavy load, but he could be a force to be reckoned with in his own right.

Ain't no could be about it, stud. You are a force. My force.

Only because of you. Deka had helped him find that core of strength in him, reminded him of who he could be. Also helped him find what little honor he had left.

Now, he stood at the head of an army. A dragon army, an array of cryptozoids and even humans the likes of which the world had never seen.

And they were impressive. Him most of all.

Samael wore black robes edged in silver, the

needlework perfect, the runes ancient but cool looking. He drew the line at the staff and beard Deka had insisted on.

Spoilsport.

At his side, the Golden king wore a splendid military uniform, hand stitched by the best seamstresses, and ornate enough to befit a king.

The king's advisors and generals—the head of the Septs, with the Silvers being the most prominent—had all chosen to wear their house colors along with stoic expressions, their faces masks carved from stone. But their eyes…they glowed green with excitement.

It had been a while since dragons were able to openly fight.

Behind the governing ranks lined the army. Most had eschewed uniforms to emerge as their other selves.

Dragons with scales gleaming in the dawning sun. Heads held high, and in their clawed fists, weapons—pole arms, and spears, plus modern-day tools finely calibrated to each warrior. In the olden days they eschewed weapons, thinking claws and teeth were enough. Arrogance had helped to kill them.

They'd adapted. They created their own line of dragon-friendly weapons. And now, they'd finally get to baptize them with enemy blood.

Weapons weren't the only change in this battle. Armor encased them, made to protect their more vulnerable bellies. Many wore helmets to protect their heads.

A fierce-looking troop.

The shapeshifters roamed restlessly, their furry minds eager for the chase while the humans among them fidgeted, their fingers sweaty on the stocks of their guns. The human governments had sent their soldiers to fight and never asked what they thought. They'd sent their fragile men and women to stand awed and honored among monsters of legend.

It was a glorious army. A beautiful militia.

And the whole world got to see it because some news network morons were actually standing nearby, broadcasting.

"How has the human race survived this long?" Samael muttered.

"They procreate like rabbits," was Zahra's reply.

Can you both zip it? I'm trying to look menacing here. Remiel spoke in their minds rather than aloud, probably because a dark cloud on the horizon approached, the opposing army of darkness.

Deka suddenly spoke to him. *Wait, that would make us the army of light. I totally chose the wrong outfit for this.*

Her priorities were as skewed as ever. No surprise she'd chosen to join him in this final battle.

As if she'd stay behind, when, in her words, "But this girl just wants to have fun." She'd even sung that to him over and over and over until he agreed—the blowjob helped make her case.

Having her here was actually a good thing. It meant Samael couldn't fail. Because failure would mean her getting hurt, and he had made a promise to never let that happen.

Plus, the caterers were waiting just over the dunes to set up and get the party going.

Before this day ended, Deka would be his wife.

Cocky muffin. I like it.

Her encouragement wasn't needed to bolster

him, not anymore. He'd found his balls and yanked them free. But the praise did fire him hotter. *Once this battle is over, I'm claiming my princess.*

Charge! Yeah, that was his impatient fiancée who yelled it in his head. He used magic to snare her before she could ruin his plan.

Let me go, stud. I can take her.

No, she couldn't. None of them were strong enough to fight the witch. Not even Samael.

Which was why this had to be done just right.

The opposing army stopped yards away, and Voa stepped forward, her tightly fitted gown of red a slap to the Crimsons that she'd fooled and manipulated.

She walked toward them, slow and undulating. Wasted. There was nothing attractive about her.

Remiel strode forward to meet her, Samael two steps behind. The air already held hints of dusty heat, the acrid kind without a hint of moisture.

That would change as blood was spilled.

Think I can get a shot? Remiel asked without moving his lips.

"A fatal one? Nope." There was only one way to end this according to the Jabbas. The question was, did he trust them?

They stopped while still several yards away from Voa. Out of physical reach but close enough to hear each other.

"How nice of you all to gather in one place for capture." Her rapacious smile held a hint of darkness.

"Ditto to your army. It will make it easier for me to eliminate them."

"You think vanquishing them will make a difference?" Voa angled her head. "Do you really think I need these puny creatures to achieve my victory?"

"Obviously, you need help, or you would have come alone. I guess you're not that strong, after all."

Her lips flattened. "I see what you are doing. Thinking I'll lose my temper and send them away."

"Please, don't," Samael interjected. "Deka's been looking forward to this fight. She'll be pissed if she doesn't get to spill any blood."

His words drew Voa's attention. "And there is the one who thinks he can beat me." Her lips pulled into a sneer. "Your magic is but a tiny spark to my inferno."

"Sometimes you only need a spark to start a fire."

The laughter emerged discordant and false. "You'll soon see what true power is. It will amuse me to have you both kneeling at my feet. Swearing fealty and then feeding me as part of your surrender."

"Blah blah blah. Can we get on with the fighting already?" someone yelled from the waiting army.

"You heard my people." Remiel shrugged. "They are raring to kick your ass."

"Today, the reign of dragons ends, and a new world order will—"

The aim of whoever lobbed the egg was good. It hit Voa in the chest and splattered.

As to why there was an egg?

All part of the plan.

Voa screeched, and her face pulsed, her skin rippling and bulging as if something crawled under it.

Something did. Darkness.

Also known as a spell gone wrong. Over and over again. It appeared Voa had sucked dry one too many bodies. She bore the signs of a body overindulging. Yes, the souls made her strong, but they changed her, too. Changed her in ways that weren't healthy.

For them.

While freaky and somewhat possessed, she was almost invincible.

Almost.

Voa lifted from the ground, her gown fluttering as she elevated herself, arms spread widely as she intoned in a deep voice, "Attack."

Kind of anticlimactic.

Remiel, for his part, muttered for his mind alone, *Ready, brother?*

As ready as he could be when pitting his strength against that of a psychotic, ancient sorceress.

You can do this, muffin.

While appreciated, her faith wasn't needed. Not anymore. *I will do this.*

As Remiel launched himself into the air, shredding his fine-stitched clothes, Samael kept an eye on the sun.

The timing had to be just right.

The roar of battle echoed over the desert sand as the armies raced toward each other, determined to shed blood. Those with guns got an early start, and the sharp crackle and pop of bullets being fired filled the air with noise and the acrid stench of gun smoke.

Remiel played with Voa, who rippled into a perverted hybrid form, bloated beyond belief, and holy shit, there were tentacles coming out of the tips of her legs.

Moving quickly, a gleam of gold zipping and twirling, Remiel kept out of reach of Voa while landing the occasional shot, the lobbed balls of golden energy that did nothing but make the mutant sorceress madder.

A glint of silver overhead drew his attention as Deka met a smaller green dragon—one that subverted to the other side—head-on. They grappled in the air, his princess choking on the fumes the vapor dragon breathed. But her mother had protected Deka well. The potions Xylia had fed the army wouldn't last long, but hopefully, it would be long enough to repel the poisons and vanquish those spraying them.

The sky turned dark, and not just because of the bodies crowding it fighting for their lives. The moon had begun to cross over the sun. The propitious eclipse that would save their asses was beginning, which meant Samael needed to roll up his sleeves and start, too.

He closed his eyes, shutting out the sounds of battle, dropping into the meditative zone the Jabba brothers had taught him—*Clear your mind.* Slap. *Clear it means not thinking of a woman.* Slap.

It took quite a few cuffs upside the head before Samael learned to remove all distractions from his thoughts.

The world outside disappeared, and he opened his inner eye to see the zinging lines of power that intersected everything.

Bright spots of light for life, shiny threads for the power that crisscrossed the plain, and a pulsing dark spot for the abomination that was Voa.

And then there was—

Something knocked him out of his trance, and he hit the ground hard, the slavering jaws of a werewolf gone mad inches from his face.

Before he could pulverize it with magic, the wolf was plucked from him and twisted. *Crack.*

The limp body got tossed, and Deka reached

down to haul him to his feet. Her silver dragon towered over his human shape.

The other side of him yearned to join her, yet he couldn't. For this spell, he needed fingers.

He also needed no more interruptions. The moon was almost over the sun. He needed to work the spell.

Do what you have to, stud muffin. I'll stand guard.

And he knew she would guard him with her life. *Because she's my mate.*

Damned straight I am, muffin, so get going on the magic stuff so we can get to the wedding stuff.

He knelt on the ground this time, his fingertips pressed in to the dirt, and shuttered his mind, quickly finding his place again, seeing the threads, insignificant strands.

It was almost time.

Ready yourself, brother. He shouted it mentally and hoped Remiel heard. As the moon fully covered the sun, he blinked his second set of lids and drew upon his othersight. It showed things in a different light. Illuminated the magic.

A thick cord of red speared down to the earth, a bull's-eye from the eclipse. He shoved his fist into the glow and tugged. He twirled the strand of magic in the dirt, swirled and twirled, wider and wider.

The ground underneath trembled.

Impressive. The only magic he'd learned because, as the Jabbas told him, *You don't have time to catch up to her level of skill. So you need to trick her.*

The hole, once started, kept widening. Things fell into it. Bodies. Dead and alive. The screams haunting.

A set of claws yanked him back before the earth at his feet crumbled away.

Opening his eyes, he felt more than saw the hole he'd ripped open. Pure darkness lay over the land as the eclipse stole the light from the world.

An ominous Ohm-ing sound came from the interdimensional rip, and he stumbled back with Deka.

The time was here. He shouted, "Now! Do it now."

Despite the gloom, Remiel's gold scales flashed in the sky, and all saw the golden fire as it emerged from his mouth and struck a very distorted Voa.

She screamed as her flesh melted and reformed, and melted again to form again, the souls she'd imbibed keeping her alive. Kind of cool that she got to suffer over and over. Even better, it distracted her enough she didn't know she was being pushed.

But she wasn't arriving fast enough. Time ticked. Precious time.

Samael extended his hands and grabbed hold of her dark magic, feeling it slither through his hands, slimy and gross, yet he reeled it in, drawing her closer to the abyss he'd created.

She paused in her struggle as she finally saw the hole. "Is that your plan? Shove me into another dimension? I'll just come right back." As if to mock him, she hovered over the hole, laughing.

A tentacle covered in suckers with stingers in the middle whipped out of the rip and wrapped around her ankles. With a yank, it drew her down.

Eyes wide.

Mouth open.

A short-lived scream.

The massive kraken-like creature the Jabbas had told him about, the one that could rarely be summoned, who wasn't content with just one witch.

One witch isn't even a snack.

More tentacles whipped out and snared those closest. One even wrapped around Deka and began to pull.

Without thinking, Samael slashed down with his hand, severing it with magic. Then and only then did he finally shift into his dragon and pull Deka away from the abyss.

Go back. I think we can take it.

We can't go into that world. There is no way back. And the current passageway was about to close.

The moon moved past the sun, and as light dawned once again on the land, the hole in the ground shrank. The tentacles shriveled as the rays of light struck them.

With a piercing scream that shook the very air, the alien creature withdrew its appendages. The hole shrank and shrank.

It was barely large enough for a person when fingers appeared on the edge, humanoid fingers that scrabbled for the sides.

A silver dragon landed by the hand, looking for purchase. Zahra transformed and gave a haughty look to the digits before stomping on them.

Crunch. Pop. The hand was gone, the hole, too.

The dragons had won the day!

Without their leader and the mind control, the other side collapsed. Running, wailing, begging for their lives.

Cowards. Not worth his time. Samael ignored them all. He looked at his Silver princess and fluted a query. *Ready to get mated?*

Chapter Twenty-three

It's my wedding day!

With Suzie sucked into another dimension that could only be opened during an eclipse in that exact location—which meant Suzie was fucked for a super long time, if she even managed to survive the tentacle monster—they could all relax.

The world had been saved by dragons.

In time, because history tended to repeat itself, the humans would resent the dragons for helping. Those short lived, fragile creatures hated being beholden, but at the same time, they couldn't exactly declare war on a superior species. They could, however, cough up some serious cash and concessions. Already there were plans to form a group that would address the needs of dragons and how they could cohabit with humanity—so that they could eventually rule them. Part of the long-term game involved infiltrating all levels of government thus ensuring their protection and dominance.

Deka really didn't give a damn about the politics or repercussions of the battle that day.

She was getting married!

Samael had planned it all. Actually, what he'd done in man fashion was tell her mother.

"I'm marrying Deka right after the fight. If you want her in a dress with flowers and shit, then make it happen

because I'm not waiting any longer."

It was stupidly romantic, and a challenge no dragon mother could refuse. Mother was up to the task.

Deka walked down the beach—after everyone went for a cleansing dip—in a lovely white gown, her feet bare in the sand, her hair woven with colorful flowers, and her smile so bright she could have been Elspeth's sister.

Samael had changed into a tux, but was also barefoot in the warm sand. His golden hair had a shade of something darker to it, and his eyes glowed, more red than green now. As for his forehead, maybe he wouldn't notice the lumps in their wedding pictures.

But she didn't mind. He was special. *And mine.*

Her cousins Adi and Aimee acted as bridesmaids, and, of course, Babette was the moping maid of honor—although that lip didn't hang for long. Deka had seen a lovely pale blue water dragon giving her best friend the eye. If that could turn to tongue, Babette would soon be on the mend.

Walking past rank after rank, she noted with deep satisfaction that the crowd was immense. Dragons and allies alike filling the sandy aisles, most waiting for the boring ceremony part to be done so they could eat. The smells from the barbecue pits wafted, making more than one tummy growl.

Finally, she arrived, the heat and tingle of her muffin reaching out to wrap around her.

Before she could go to him, her mother kissed her lightly on the cheek murmuring, "May you always be happy, or I'll rip out his guts."

Deka sniffled. It was so beautiful. Looking up, she smiled at Samael. She couldn't help the radiance.

He looked so magnificent. *I love him so much.*

I love you, too.

At that point, once he said those words, aliens could have landed, and she wouldn't have blinked.

As it was, it was a good thing Samael took her hand and held it as they turned to face Remiel together. His brother presided over the ceremony, wearing an ornate crown and embroidered stole, his white suit threaded in gold.

"We are gathered here today to join this dragon and this dragoness in a holy mating. And let me tell you, I never thought that would happen. My brother and I haven't always had the easiest relationship—"

Someone muttered, "Understatement."

"—yet, today I am filled with great joy and honor that we've managed to overcome our difficulties to vanquish a mighty foe."

"Did he say ho?" someone whispered.

"Let today be the new dawn where magic once again takes its rightful place instead of being banished. Let us work together for a future where dragons and cryptozoids no longer have to hide in shadows, and where our future heirs"—he cast a loving glance over at his wife Sue-Ellen, who sat in the crowd holding her rounded belly—"don't have to fear being hunted. Today, we don't just join this man and woman, we didn't just defeat the greatest evil of our time, today dawns a new era. The era of dragons."

A roar of approval met his speech, and Deka clung tightly to Samael's hand. Their wedding day would go down in history.

Best present ever.

"And now on to the ceremony. Do you, Samael D'Ore, take Deka Silvergrace as your mate?

Do you promise to protect and hoard her until the end of your life?"

"I do."

As for Deka, she couldn't wait. "I do, too. Get to the good part."

Remiel smiled. "Before the eyes of all, let it be known that these two claim each other and should any try to tear them asunder—"

"We'll rip out their eyes and stomp on their guts." More than a few voices shouted it, and Deka almost cried again.

"Then, by the power vested in me, as king of all dragons, I pronounce thee mated for life. You may place the marks."

Samael drew her close and brushed her lips before sliding his mouth to her neck. An ecstatic gasp escaped her lips as he bit the skin, hard enough to break it and spill blood. She returned the favor, making his mark high enough to never be hidden by any collar.

Let the heifers see he belonged to her. Let everyone see she'd claimed him.

No longer did they have to hide the symbol of their mating from those who didn't understand.

A new era would dawn, and it would be glorious.

So will the orgasm I give you later.

Epilogue

Orgasms could only happen so many times before they lost a little of their power.

Despite her best attempts to keep Samael naked, even Deka couldn't make their honeymoon last forever, especially after the most recent luxury hotel kicked them out for excessive noise complaints.

"Bunch of uptight biddies," she grumbled. "I can't control how loud I scream when I come."

"Obviously. I'm just that good."

So good. Samael was also good at arguing, which led to the dropped charges of indecent public affection.

The only thing indecent about it was the cop who stopped them before they got to the fun part.

Real life called, usually in the form of her mother with her daily question of, "Did he get you pregnant yet?" Someone was anxious to be a grandma.

They returned to the Underground Lair of Deviousness—a title Samael begrudgingly allowed. Secretly, she was convinced he loved it. After all, he was her evil overlord and—

"I'm not evil," he remarked as he carried his wife—*that's me!*—over the threshold.

"Can't you be just a tiny bit evil, for me?" she asked.

He sighed, and she thought he was about to agree, only he said, "Would it kill you to call first?"

As to whom Samael spoke to, it was Remiel, dressed casually, leaning in the doorway to the living room—which had better have been redecorated in that under the sea theme she'd ordered.

"I thought we should speak in person."

"As long as it's only speaking." Deka shoved out of his grip and stood in front of Samael, every inch of her bristling. "Don't you even think of killing my husband. He's mine, and I won't let you hurt him."

Adorable and emasculating at the same time. But to love Deka was to accept that she would never sit gracefully in the background.

"No one is killing anyone. Not yet."

"I should hope not," Samael grumbled. "He's drinking my oldest scotch. It would be a waste."

She eyed Remiel suspiciously. "Why are you here then? Do you need us to vanquish evil again? Did you have another wedding gift?"

"Actually, I'm here to give Samael a more official title than brother. I know we've had our differences, and don't have the warmest relationship."

"Arctic," Deka coughed into her fist.

"But I'd like us to put that aside and work together to—"

"Make the world a better place," she sang.

"Actually, I was going to say rule it. I'm only one dragon, and I could use someone I can trust at my back. The humans can't be trusted to protect our interests. Which means we'll need to step up. What do you say?" Remiel held out his hand, and Samael stared at it.

Overwhelmed, the poor guy. So Deka grabbed

his hand and shoved it into his brother's. "He accepts. So long as he gets to make his headquarters here. Oh, and we want a cool title."

"How's the King's First Advisor and Senior Wizard sound?"

"I'm your only wizard."

"It comes with a staff of Silvers to boss around."

Samael's hand tightened on his brother's. "I won't let you down."

You'd better not. Our child deserves only the very best.

Samael whirled. "You're…"

"Very pregnant. *Daddy.*"

Good thing Remiel was there to catch him before he smashed his pretty face.

And she captured it all on video and added it to her hoard. She'd begun a new section in it, one dedicated to the wonderful life she'd started with Samael. Because now that her dragon was reborn, she didn't want to miss a single moment.

***

The walk was longer than they liked, but they were left no choice.

The hell dimension portal to Earth was busted. Samael might have gifted the brothers with freedom by setting them free on this plane, but he wouldn't give them access to his.

"And he's supposed to be the future of our kind?" Maedoc snorted. "How did it not occur to him that there was more than one place in this world to cross over?"

"Because we never told him," replied Eogan with a smirk.

There were many things they'd omitted telling Samael and his concubine, such as exactly how they'd deciphered the ancient language in the texts they found.

None of them could read the language. Good thing the inhabitants here could and welcomed those exiled with open arms.

It was kind of sad when they eventually disappeared. The start of their slow tumble.

Now, unless they moved their asses and acted, they would finally come to the end of their life.

We did not fight this hard to stay alive to die now. Not when freedom was so close.

"Good thing we had that snack stashed away."

Voadicia wasn't the only one who'd benefitted from being so close to earthside. When they went and collected dragons for her use, the Jabbas bargained for extra for them. And hid them. They couldn't suck at their souls much without notifying the suzerain they'd been feeding.

But with her and the Golden apprentice gone, they siphoned as quickly as they could before making the journey to the other citadel.

It took more than a few souls to change their amorphous slob shape. They'd regained their trim stature. Their lush hair, and their mischievous nature.

We're back.

Maedoc snickered. He'd watched the same movie and recognized the accent.

Now able to fit in, they were ready to cross over one last time. The dimensions were shifting. Soon, they would be out of sync. They couldn't delay any longer, yet they couldn't help but pause before a door leading down to a very well-protected dungeon in a castle far, far away from their usual home. A dungeon with only a single occupant in it. One not visited in quite some time.

Because the suzerain thought the occupant dead.

"Should we?" asked Maedoc.

Eogan looked at the barred door and thought of what lay beyond. "He is likely to be imbued with a murderous rage."

"Yup."

"It seems only right we free him, too." Especially after what they'd done.

The lock disengaged, and they fled, off to start their new and wondrous—ly wicked—lives.

As to the one locked away for all those centuries, born in captivity because his world was invaded and his people killed until only he remained?

He stepped out of his cell for the first time since his birth. He might have rejoiced except, what was there to celebrate?

His world was dead. The lushness of it killed by the dragons who had siphoned every ounce of life from the land.

There is nothing for me here. Nothing but the bitter taste and smell of defeat.

With only one purpose, he followed the tracks of the ones who'd set him free, followed them to an ancient portal created by his people. A peaceful race overcome by the greed of dragons.

But I am not my ancestors. He wouldn't meekly bend a knee and accept his fate. He wanted vengeance, and he could only achieve that elsewhere.

Inhaling deeply, he took a look back at the castle, seen for the first time in person—yet familiar because his mother used to share images of it with him as a child cradled on her lap.

And then she died.

They all died.

A family that stretched generations, going from violent and war mongering to peaceful. And easily destroyed.

Turning away from the physical reminder of their defeat, he took a step through the portal and choked as he breathed fresh air for the first time.

The sweetness brought tears to his eyes. The purity dropped him to his knees with weakness. He bowed his head as he finally understood exactly what had been taken from him.

Everything.

Standing on the parapet of the crumbling castle, he surveyed the land he'd come to. Lush. Green. Alive…

Mine. The dragons had taken everything in his world. It seemed only fair that he return the favor.

Soon, you will know my name. You will fear it.

My name is Lucifer, the last branch of the Shining Ones. And this world is about to become mine.

The End… Nah. Next up is Demon Walking.

For more Eve Langlais books and news visit EveLanglais.com

CPSIA information can be obtained
at www.ICGtesting.com
Printed in the USA
LVOW12s1503261217
560794LV00001BA/144/P

9 781988 328706